# The Praying Sk and Other Stc

Ralph Delahaye Paine

## Alpha Editions

This edition published in 2024

ISBN 9789361475139

Design and Setting By

**Alpha Editions**

www.alphaedis.com

Email - info@alphaedis.com

As per information held with us this book is in Public Domain.
This book is a reproduction of an important historical work.
Alpha Editions uses the best technology to reproduce historical work
in the same manner it was first published to preserve its original nature.
Any marks or number seen are left intentionally to preserve.

# Contents

| | |
|---|---|
| THE PRAYING SKIPPER | - 1 - |
| II | - 3 - |
| III | - 7 - |
| IV | - 11 - |
| V | - 14 - |
| A VICTORY UNFORESEEN | - 22 - |
| II | - 29 - |
| III | - 31 - |
| IV | - 35 - |
| V | - 38 - |
| VI | - 40 - |
| VII | - 43 - |
| VIII | - 46 - |
| CORPORAL SWEENEY, DESERTER | - 51 - |
| THE LAST PILOT SCHOONER | - 67 - |
| THE JADE TEAPOT | - 84 - |
| CAPTAIN ARENDT'S CHOICE | - 96 - |
| SURFMAN BRAINARD'S "DAY OFF" | - 109 - |

# THE PRAYING SKIPPER

"But I'm not going to stand for this sort of thing," angrily protested young Valentine as he shoved the letter at Port Captain Graham of the Palmetto Line. "The old man may be as good a sailor as you say he is, but it's high time we set him ashore on a half-pay pension. Why, he's making our service ridiculous. Read it out to Mr. Holmes."

The Port Captain fidgeted and awkwardly wiped his glasses, for the task was unwelcome:

DEAR VALENTINE: Congratulations on your decision to mix up in the business of the old company. It seems a hefty responsibility for so young a man, but blood will tell. By the way, here is something for you to investigate while the new broom is sweeping the cobwebs away. I went South on your *Suwannee* a month ago, and have the honor to inform you that her captain is a venerable nuisance, and loose in his top story. He is a religious crank, clean dippy on it, held prayer-meetings until half the passengers were driven on deck, and had a lot of hysterical women flocking around him for two different services on Sunday. The *Suwannee* is a gospel ark in command of a praying skipper, and if only the sanctified are going to enjoy traveling in her, you will lose a lot of business. I reckon it's time the line had an overhauling, so good luck to you.

    Yours as ever,

                    Jim.

Young Mr. Valentine explained to the surprised officials:

"The signer is an old college friend of mine, man of a great deal of influence here in New York, and he gives the line and its biggest, newest ship this kind of a black eye. And I have heard other rumors to the same effect. Now I want an explanation from both you gentlemen. You know all about Captain Jesse Kendrick of the *Suwannee*, and it's your business to report such idiotic performances. If you have been shielding a dottering old ass, who is unfit to go to sea any longer, the sooner the thing is sifted to the bottom the better."

Port Captain Graham flushed and twisted his white mustache with a fist like an oaken billet. He swallowed hard as if trying to keep his rising steam under control, and replied with a catch in his deep voice:

"Mr. Valentine, I've been with the Palmetto Line going on thirty years, from the time when your father bought the first old side-wheeler that flew the house flag. Jesse Kendrick was third under me in my first command and I know him inside out. A finer sailor and a better man never rounded Hatteras. Are you going to blackguard the ranking skipper afloat in your service because of a flimsy complaint like that, without calling the old man up to the office? Doesn't he get a hearing? Why, you've just now waltzed into this company like a boy with a lot of toy steamboats to play with, after loafing abroad in a muck of luxury ever since you left your college. You've never even clapped eyes on Captain Kendrick."

Mr. Holmes, the General Manager, was speaking before Mr. Valentine could make heated reply. He was largely office bred, and less outspoken than the rugged Port Captain:

"As far as his religion goes, we know that Captain Kendrick doesn't drink a drop, and that he won't ship anything but sober men. And your father had reason to send the old man a good many letters of commendation in his time. Shall I 'phone to the dock for Captain Kendrick? He sails this afternoon."

"You'll do nothing of the kind," snarled Valentine. "I'll do my own investigating this time, because you are a bunch of three old pals, do you see?"

"But you're not going to censure him right off the reel? Good God! it would break the old man's heart," exclaimed the Port Captain, leaning forward in a bluster of indignation. "I'll bet the morals of your friend, Jim What's-his-name, need investigatin' a damn sight more than the righteousness of Jesse Kendrick."

Mr. Valentine snapped back, but with weakening assurance:

"If you can't be civil, Captain Graham, there will be more than one reprimand in this day's work. I am the owner ashore, and I propose to be the boss at sea. I'll think it over, and if I want any more of your advice, I'll send for you. Good-morning."

He went into an inner office and closed the door. The Port Captain glared at the barrier, and growled as he trudged reluctantly into the outer hall, arm in arm with the General Manager.

"*That* spindle-shouldered, under-engined young cub as the make-believe boss of the Palmetto Line! What do you think of it, Holmes? Dyin' must have come hard to his dad when he took a last squint at the heir to the business. This one surely needs some of Jesse Kendrick's spare prayers."

"The young Valentine is cock of the walk," said the General Manager slowly. "But the bantam was crowing to show his authority this time. Anyhow, he said he would think it over, and that means he'll cool off.

Don't say anything to Kendrick about it. No use of discounting trouble that may never come."

But the two men had small acquaintance with the methods of young Mr. Valentine. Without letting go his purpose, he had appeared to give way, because he shrunk from pitting his will against this masterful Port Captain, who made him feel like a house of cards in a big wind. It was not inconceivable that this over-bearing old monster might lay him across his knee and spank him in the white heat of a dispute. When he heard the two veterans depart, the new-fledged owner turned to his stenographer:

"Please take a letter to Captain Kendrick and mail it to catch him at New Orleans. I don't want him storming in here to-day."

The gray hair of the stenographer had been a bonny brown when she entered the employ of the Palmetto Line. As her pencil chased his words down the pages of her notebook, she glanced up with undisguised amazement, and dared to comment when her task was done:

"Please pardon me, but are you sure you mean Captain Kendrick of the *Suwannee*? You see, I have sailed with him on several vacation trips. When he leads the services on board, I think it is because the passengers like to hear him talk; such manly, honest talk about the faith he lives day by day. He reminds you of some Old Testament patriarch."

"Old Testament patriarchs are out of date," said Mr. Valentine with evident irritation. "Is there a conspiracy to boom the stock of this senile old geezer? Religion is all right for you women. I am going South in my private car next week, and by Jove, I will just come home on the *Suwannee* and look the situation over for myself. Mum's the word. And I don't want any more of my friends to be guying me about running a marine Sunday-school with a sea-parson in charge. That letter ought to choke him off coming back."

## II

A fortnight later the *Suwannee* was steaming across the sapphire Gulf. Before her bow flying-fish skittered and splashed like flights of shrapnel bullets, on deck sailors were stretching awnings fore and aft, and wind-sails bellied in the open hatches. Men in flannels and women in trim, white freshness leaned along the rail and watched the sparkling play of color overside. There was the air of a yachting cruise in these pleasant aspects of the day's routine, yet the season was the dead of winter, and the *Suwannee* was hurrying as fast as twin screws could drive her toward bitter latitudes.

On the bridge walked to and fro, with a slightly limping gait, a man of an unusual presence. Those who looked up at him from the deck noted his uncommon height and breadth, and the white beard that swept almost to his waist. Nearer vision was needed to know the seamed yet mobile face, and the gray eye that held an eager light as of strong emotions continually burning. When he halted to speak to his first officer, his voice was sweet and vibrant:

"I am going below for a little while, Mr. Parlin. Call me when you've run down your course."

Captain Kendrick went into his room just abaft the wheelhouse, and picked up from his desk a typewritten letter that showed marks of much handling. He read it slowly, and his lip quivered as it had done with each of many previous readings. Seating himself upon the edge of the couch, he said aloud little fragments of the letter, taken here and there without sequence:

"Astonishing behavior ... guilty of annoyance ... serious complaints ... ridiculous religious display ... prime of usefulness past ... evidently ripe for retirement...."

The letter fell to the floor unheeded, as there came into his eyes a look of impassioned intensity that was focused ever so far beyond the walls of this little sea-cabin. He was on his knees and his head was in his hands as he murmured:

"Cast me not off in the time of old age, forsake me not when my strength faileth.... Thy way is in the sea, and Thy path in the great waters.... I said I will keep my mouth with a bridle while the wicked are before me. But it is also written that evening and morning and at noon will I pray and cry aloud and He shall hear my voice.... They have prepared a net for my steps, my heart is bowed down.... But Thou hast a mighty arm, strong is Thy hand and high is Thy right hand...."

While Captain Kendrick was voicing his troubles and his consolations in words wondrously framed by another strong man long ago, the purser of the *Suwannee* was sought out by Arthur Valentine, whose manner held a trace of uneasiness. He would not have confessed it, but far back in the young ship-owner's head was the glimmering notion that a terrier might be snapping at a mastiff. Was this imposing figure on the bridge the "dottering ass" to whom he had smartly dashed off his first official reprimand, gloating in the chance to test the sweep of his new authority? But this suspicion now shaped itself only in a growing fear lest he be discovered in such uncomfortably close quarters with Captain Jesse Kendrick. Mr. Valentine closed the door of the purser's room and set that worthy officer's teeth on edge by remarking:

"Fine morning. I say, you needn't bother to make any special point of seating me at the captain's table. Fact is, I don't want to be bored. Just put me over at your table, will you? And please tell nobody who I am. I want to look around a bit. The captain doesn't know that I'm on board, I take it, or he would have been showing me some troublesome attentions. So you need say nothing to him about it. Just see that my name is rubbed off his copy of the passenger list."

The purser disentangled himself from a staggering heap of cargo manifests, and emphasized his reply with a wave of an inky finger:

"All right, Mr. Valentine, if those are your orders, but you miss your guess if you think our skipper is going to run after you or any other passenger. He ain't that kind. But sub rosy you go and as far as you like, till further notice."

Slightly ruffled, Mr. Valentine sauntered on deck, where he fell in with Second-Officer Peter Carr, who proved to be contrastingly voluble and cheerful. Before the passenger could ask certain questions that were in his mind, Mr. Carr flourished an arm seaward, and began:

"Passin' that bark yonder reminds me of a voyage I sailed as bos'n in the old packet *Guiding Star*, out o' Liverpool for Sydney. We was carryin' two hundred Irish girls as immygrants, an' soon after we crossed the Line they mutinied 'cause we refused to give 'em curlin' irons, an' let 'em waltz with the sailors every night an' twice on Sunday. 'Bout four bells of the middle watch pourin' out o' the hatches they come like a consolidated female explosion. I was in th' waist, an' fust I knowed them millions of infuriated young angels surged straight at poor Peter Carr. Sez I to myself, here's too much of a good thing for once, an' with that I makes a flyin' scoot an' scrambles aloft like a cat with a bunch o' firecrackers belayed to its spanker boom. Sw-o-o-o-s-h, the rustle of them billion o' skirts is like the sound of a nor'easter. Wh-e-e-e-e, them shrieks of disapp'inted rage is still ringin' in my ears. I seen the poor old skipper poke his head out o' the companionway, an' so help me, before he had time to say——"

Mr. Carr stopped abruptly and his animated countenance froze in horror as he saw Captain Kendrick wave a beckoning hand from far forward.

"He's got me again," muttered the mate, as he obeyed the summons and was seen to follow the cause of his panic into the captain's room.

"Sit down, Mr. Carr," said Captain Kendrick, with a menacing note in his voice. "You have broken your solemn promise made to me last voyage. Those same old gestures told me you were climbing the shrouds of the *Guiding Star* again. How often have I got to tell you that the *Guiding Star* packet foundered a dozen years before you went to sea? You soft-shelled coaster, you wouldn't know the equator if it flew up and hit you in the nose. 'When you were crossing the Line'—lies, all lies!"

Peter Carr rubbed his red head and looked sheepish. "Right you are, sir. I forgot, sir," he stammered. "But I'm improvin'. I can feel it workin'."

"It isn't only your speech and conduct that need overhauling," commented Captain Kendrick severely, as he dug his two fists into his beard and towered over the contrite mate. "These things are signs of an inward state of spiritual rottenness, and I intend to hammer the blessed truth into you as long as we are shipmates. Look at me. Am I a worse sailor for trying to be what your mother on Cape Cod prayed you might grow into, when she used to tuck you up in bed?"

Mr. Carr was as earnest as ever in his turbulent career as he responded:

"I'll keep in mind what you say, sir. If all the people that flies church colors was like you, a —— —— sight more of 'em 'ud practice what they preach. Whoa, Bill, I didn't mean to rip out them naughty words. I swear I didn't, sir."

The old man sighed:

"You're still in the mire. But I'm not done with you. I'll have you on your knees yet, Peter Carr."

As the mate rolled forward he muttered:

"He's sometimes kind of wearin', but he means well. An' he's gettin' me so tame I'll be eatin' out of his hand before long."

Arthur Valentine was hovering within ear-shot, and he halted the solemn-faced officer with:

"Sorry you couldn't finish that bully yarn of the *Guiding Star*. Anything the matter? How did you escape from the two hundred angry ladies?"

Mr. Carr beamed with animation as he hastened to reply: "Well, as I was sayin', the poor old skipper of her stuck his head on deck, an' before he could— Oh, d— Ouch, excuse me. I bit my tongue. I mean, well, I never did get down out of that riggin', and that's the end of the yarn. Can't explain. No time to talk now."

Valentine was puzzled, and laid a hand on the sleeve of the fleeing mate:

"What the dickens ails you? Why can't you finish that yarn?"

Mr. Carr whipped round and shouted with a noble impulse:

"I ain't goin' to lie again, so help me. The captain's been laborin' with my poor sin-streaked soul, and I passed the word to steer by his sailin' chart. I've suffered enough without bein' keel-hauled any more about it."

"Beg pardon," smiled Valentine. "Now I see the joke. The good old man and the wandering boy. How nice of him. Perhaps he will pray for me if I send up a card. Is he often taken that way?"

"Pretty regular," grinned the mate as he made good his retreat.

"Was I right? Well, rather," thought Valentine. "It's time I took hold of things. If we should run into a storm, the old duffer would be on his knees praying for good weather and let the ship go to pot."

Later in the day a notice posted in the "social hall" caught his roving eye:

"To-morrow (Sunday) divine service will be held in the main saloon at ten o'clock. As is customary in steamers of this line when there is no clergyman among the passengers, the captain will be in charge of this service."

### III

Four bells on Sunday morning found the saloon half filled with voyagers, most of whom looked as if church-going was their custom. Sunlight flooded through the open ports and fretted the floor with dancing patterns as the steamer rolled lazily with the weight of the breathing sea. A warm wind gushed under the skylights and brought with it the thankful twitter of a little brown land-bird blown into the rigging over night. If ever worship were meet at sea, a singular aptness was in the peace and brightness of this place.

A hymn was sung and the captain read the morning service from the prayer-book. Then he threw back his shoulders without knowing that he did so, until the blue uniform coat stretched very taut across his bulky chest, and his corded hand gripped a small Bible that lay before him. Something in his pose told those of quick intuition that big emotions were hard held. They knew not why, but this hoary pillar of a man was tugging at their sympathies even before he began to speak, at first frowningly, then with a gathering light in his rugged face:

"From time to time I have tried to make these shipboard services a little more than the routine calls for. It was my way of thinking that when the Lord has led a man up out of the pit, and planted his feet on the Rock, he ought not to be ashamed of it. Perhaps I have had pride in my redemption. But it seemed to me a wonderful thing that a wicked, drunken young sailor, with no mother and no home, should be brought up with a round turn, as by a miracle of grace; that like a great light shining on the deep waters, the new hope of a better, manlier life came to him; and that he found the peace that passeth all understanding. Since then, some men and women have told me that they remembered sailing with me long after the voyage was done.

"Now I can speak no more of these things. This may be my last voyage, and if I were to talk to you out of the fullness of my heart it would be wrong. For the Book says, 'servants obey your masters,' and I am still a servant, wearing a servant's livery, and I have been proud to wear it for a good many years. I can't say any more. Several passengers asked me to give a talk in connection with the morning's service, and I want them to know that in disappointing them, my wishes have been overruled. Let us all thank God for fair weather in a closing hymn."

Arthur Valentine left the saloon fairly well pleased with himself, but inwardly recording one objection:

"He's pretty well muzzled, but I wrote him to cut out all his religious palaver in public, and I won't stand for any more of this nonsense of playing the martyr. That goes."

While idling forward after lunch, he met the first-officer coming off watch. Mischievous fortune thus brought together a young man with an axe to grind and a soured elder with a grievance.

"So the captain is ready to stay ashore," observed Valentine after a few greeting commonplaces. "Did you hear his queer speech this morning? I wonder what he was driving at? A passenger can't help being curious to know."

Mr. Parlin was a ripe and ruddy picture of a mariner, passing as heartily frank of speech except among those who knew him well. A lurking notion that he had seen this young man in New York was somehow coupled in his mind with the company's head offices, where an errand had called him before leaving that port. As he studied the passenger before replying, his glance was drawn to the gun-metal cigarette case, casually produced, whose face bore in gold outline the initials "A. H. V." Mr. Parlin was not dull witted. These letters stood for the name of the "old man's son."

The first-officer became inwardly alert as he said: "Well, Captain Kendrick is getting old, and he hasn't been right since he was smashed up so bad three years ago."

"How smashed?" asked Valentine eagerly.

"Got washed into the scuppers of the *Juanita*. They found him jammed under a boat with his timbers busted to smithereens. You may have noticed that he walks with a list to port."

"He didn't break his head, did he?" and Valentine tapped his forehead with a significant finger.

"Well, that's not for me to say," and Mr. Parlin hesitated, with a flutter of an eyelid; "but he has his hobby, and he sets all the sail it'll carry. You may have noticed it this morning. But he was going it very easy then."

"I'd have had my ship long before this," continued Mr. Parlin, "if the old man hadn't put a black mark on my record in the main office. Now that he talks of going out of the line, there's no harm in my sayin' that if I'd flopped on my knees and spouted psalms instead of sticking to my duties, it would be Captain Parlin by now. Excuse me. I have some work on."

Valentine said to himself as he watched the burly, bow-legged figure lumber toward a main-deck ladder:

"Now, *there's* a proper sailor for you! And this captain—pshaw, he makes me sick."

At the same time Mr. Parlin was thinking:

"Neatly done. I put a nail in the old cuss's coffin."

Three days passed before Captain Kendrick made a social appearance on the after deck. His old friends among the passengers welcomed his lavish fund of stories, some of them a trifle heavy, but all delivered with beaming good nature, and such thunderous sallies of laughter as wagged the white beard until his audience joined in from sheer sympathy. Valentine hung on the outskirts for a little while and then preferred to walk the deck. He felt irritation and disgust, partly because he thought he ought to be holding the center of the stage, and regretting that expediency should force him to travel incognito. Wouldn't these silly folk open their eyes if they knew how easily he, the owner, could lay this childish old nuisance of a skipper on the shelf? And he chafed the more because the poison so deftly administered by the first mate was working to confirm all his headlong suspicions.

Scowling at the jolly company as he passed them, Valentine caught a new note of earnestness in the captain's voice and stopped to listen:

"It may not be wrong after all, now that you are all urging me, and I will cut it short. God has been very good to me, and in my poor way I try to bear witness. And you may understand when I tell you what happened in '67 when I was battering around the fo'ksle of a deep-water ship out of Baltimore. Never will I forget the night when———"

The words produced an extraordinary effect upon Valentine. Blind anger seized him. He could see nothing else than that the captain was defying his written order, the passengers abetting him, and the whole group making a mockery of his authoritative judgment. He brushed in among the listeners, and shouted in a gusty treble:

"This has got to stop, I tell you. What did I write you, Captain Kendrick, about all this religious tommy-rot? I'll show you whose orders go on this ship."

The company scattered as if a bomb had lit in the midst of it as Captain Kendrick took two strides, whipped out a long arm and grasped Valentine by the shoulder:

"No man gives me orders on the deck of my ship at sea. Do you want to go below in irons? Who are———"

"My name is A. H. Valentine, and I threatened to kick you out of your berth two weeks ago, and you know it," screamed the struggling young man. "Turn me loose, I tell you. Pension be hanged. Now you can go ashore and rot. I own this ship and a dozen like her. I'll put the first officer in command to-day, and it's high time, too. He deserves it, and I know why he lost his promotion."

"I don't care if you're the Emperor of Chiny. Put a stopper on that tongue of yours, or—" Captain Kendrick checked his hot words and looked at the agitated young man like a pitying father. "You don't know any better, do you? We'll talk it all over ashore. But not at sea, understand—not at sea."

Captain Kendrick walked slowly toward his room without looking back, and sent word for Mr. Parlin to come to him at once. The mate breezed in with hearty salutation, but his high color paled a little when he looked squarely at the captain's flinty face.

"Stand on your two feet like a man, Mr. Parlin, for you're before your commander. Have you been telling lies to a passenger named Valentine?"

"Didn't know Mr. Valentine was aboard, sir. Wouldn't know him if he was sitting there in your chair. Are you trying to insult me?"

"Could I insult a slush-bucket?" thundered the captain. "You have been talking to Mr. Valentine. Don't spit out the lie that's on the tip of your tongue. Two years ago, I found you asleep on watch. At other times you have been slack and inefficient. I reported you every time. That's why you've seen three mates go over your head and get their ships. If I'd had my way you'd have been disrated or thrown on the beach. But you worked wires ashore, you harpooned me in the back, and you held your berth instead of being kicked out for a better man."

The mate's face was purple as he stammered:

"I haven't said anything against you, sir."

"If you're trying to work up into the wind with Mr. Valentine, you wait until you get ashore," growled the captain. "This is my ship until she docks. You can't say I ever tried to convert you to God. He doesn't want jelly-fish. He wants men."

Driven into a corner, the mate tried to take the aggressive in a burst of defiance:

"I guess that what Mr. Valentine says goes. I'll see that he hears my side of the case before sundown."

Mr. Parlin had gone too far, and he knew it before he had bitten off his empty words. Captain Kendrick jumped to his feet, and his beard was pushed within an inch of Mr. Parlin's bulbous nose:

"You're disrated now. Mr. Carr takes your berth until we make port. Get for'ard, you mutinous loafer."

"Get nothin'!" yelled Mr. Parlin. "I'm going aft to see the real boss."

Two hairy hands clamped down on his shoulders, and he was swung clear of the deck. Then his heavily shod toes beat an intermittent tattoo over the sill and along the planks, as he was hauled and shoved toward his own room. The captain shifted his burden until the mate was tucked under one arm, breathless, impotent, trickling juicy curses. He was dumped inside and heard the heavy storm-door slam and the click of a turning key before he could heave himself to his feet and hammer the barricade in useless rage until his fists bled.

## IV

Captain Kendrick had no more time to bother with such trifles as the outbreak of Valentine. Before this day had darkened the sky turned a dirty yellow, and the weight of the wind was not enough to account for the greasy, sluggish roll of the sea. The barometer needle slid unwaveringly toward the danger point, and after some uncertain shifting, the wind hauled to the northeast and grew steadily colder. Stripped of all superfluous gear on deck, the *Suwannee* was licked into fighting trim, gaunt, streaming and naked. The weeping drizzle that fogged the sky line changed to sleet, and soon after dusk came blinding snow with a great fury of wind.

When the captain faced the storm on his quivering bridge, he felt as if all breath and warmth were instantly blown out of him. No fleecy snowflakes these, but hooting volleys of icy shot, incessantly delivered. He groped along the canvased rail in a choking fight for breath until he found Mr. Carr. They gasped and flinched as they vainly tried to peer into the whirling smother.

The sea rose with incredible swiftness. Within the hour, the *Suwannee* could no longer be held on her course. Yawing wildly whenever a vicious onset of the sea smashed against her quarter and toppled on deck, the ship was brought round and hove to, dead into it. Then the racing of her screws shook her until it seemed as if the engines would tear her hull apart, and speed was slowed as much as the captain dared.

Mr. Parlin was still locked in his stateroom, and as the deep-laden *Suwannee* wrestled with the blizzard, Captain Kendrick argued in his mind whether the mutinous officer should be released at a time when all hands were sorely needed. The third officer had not been long enough promoted to shoulder any grave responsibility. In such a night as this, whose menace was hourly increasing, the vital issue was to safeguard the ship. But the captain's manhood rebelled against a compromise with his deed of clean-cut justice. And rankling in his heart was a damnable phrase, "prime of usefulness is past." It helped to give him the strength of two, now that the test had come, and he decided to fight it through with Peter Carr.

Before midnight the cold was so benumbing and deadly, without chance of respite, that freezing fast to the rail to which they clung was a fate that threatened master and mate. Each begged the other to seek a little warmth and shelter, and their indomitable wills were dead-locked time and again. At length the captain put it as a most emphatic command, and fairly hustled Peter Carr down the steps to the steam-heated wheelhouse. When the mate returned, hot with coffee and protestations that the captain take a turn below, the old man refused with a passionate gesture of finality.

Although he had striven to bank the fires of resentment, his thoughts burned like coals that callow youth, sitting in judgment, should have flung aside his faith and works together like so much trash. But never for a moment did such introspections relax his alert understanding of every symptom of the laboring tussle between ship and sea. So far she had come unhurt. Now, once, as she climbed wearily and hung for an instant like a giant see-saw, Captain Kendrick became tensely expectant as he felt through the planking a strange jarring break, somewhere down in her vitals.

Then, instead of splendidly crashing down the long slope into the hidden wrath of water, the *Suwannee* began to swing broadside as if on a pivot. The wild impulse was unchecked, even as her bow slanted into the tumbling barrier, and heaving far down to port, she rolled helpless and exposed, as a bewildered boxer drops the guard that shields his jaw from the knock-out blow.

"*Hard over, hard over,*" yelled the captain down the tube to an empty wheelhouse, for a pallid quartermaster darted from within, and scrambled to the bridge, shouting:

"She won't steer, —— —— her, she won't steer. The gear has carried away below."

With one look to windward, the captain crawled to the engine-room indicator and sent clamoring signals to reverse the port and jam full speed ahead with the starboard screw. But before the *Suwannee* could feel the altered drive of her engines, so huge a sea raced over her lurching bow that the port side of the bridge crumpled under the attack like a wire bird-cage smashed with a club. Roaring aft, the gray flood ripped a string of boats from their lashings. It left their fragments absurdly dangling from the twisted davits, and poured through the cabin skylights, whose strength collapsed like pasteboard.

Peter Carr had seen the danger in time to shout a warning as he fled to the starboard end of the bridge. On top of him came the captain, washed along in a tangle of splintered oak and canvas. The mate crawled from beneath and looked for the quartermaster. A sodden bundle of oil-skins was doubled around a stanchion almost at his feet, and life was gone from the battered features. Instinctively glancing seaward, the mate noted that the *Suwannee* had responded to the send of her screws, and was veering now to port. He signaled to ease her, and as she headed into it again, he made a rush and dragged the skipper clear. The sleeted beard was matted with blood, but the old man stirred and opened his eyes.

"We've got to nurse her along with the engines," he muttered brokenly. "Thank God for twin screws. Stand by the indicator. Sing down for hands to clear the wreckage, and overhaul the steering-gear. It felt to me like the rudder went at the pintles. But have 'em man the hand-wheel aft."

He wiped the blood from his eyes, and strove to get on his feet. One leg gave way, and he hauled himself up by gripping what was left of the rail.

"It's gone back on me again," he groaned, "but it wasn't much of a leg at best. Lend a hand, and do as I tell ye."

Peter Carr passed a lashing around the skipper's waist, and so made him fast to the steel pillar of the engine-room indicator. Now began the infinitely wary coaxing of the ship to face the storm, now with a thrust of her port screw, again with a kick of her starboard screw. It was thus she must be steered, for word came up that there was no mending the damage this side of port. The mate was afraid to take over the task of keeping the ship headed into the storm, for this was his first experience in a twin-screw steamer, yet he was as much afraid that the skipper might die if he left him where he was.

The ship fought to wrest herself free from this shifting grip, she seemed eager to slay herself by swinging to take the seas abeam, but the man whose face and beard were dappled with blotches of crimson held her hove to, as if his soul had pervaded her clanking depths. When Peter Carr implored him to have his hurts cared for, the captain answered with such shattered murmurings as these, for the cold and the pain were biting into his brain:

"But ye shall die like men, and fall like one of the princes.... Let not the water-flood overflow me, neither let the deep swallow me up.... Oh, spare me that I may recover strength before I go hence and be no more.... Then they cried unto the Lord in their trouble, and He saved them out of their distress...."

Peter Carr was a much younger man, and the violence of his exertions had so warmed his blood that he had much strength left in him. Now and then he tugged at the captain's arm, shouted in his ear, tried to lift him, and the third officer, who had come from the task of mending matters on deck, joined the heroic struggle. The captain awoke to chide them as if they were impatient boys, but his eyes saw only the swirling curtain of snow ahead and the great seas he must meet in their teeth. Suddenly he tried to stand erect, and shouted as he swayed:

"Vessel dead ahead."

With the words, he sent a signal to his engine-room, and the *Suwannee* shouldered the merest trifle off to port just as a great gray mass slid past, so close that the watchers smelled a whiff of steam. The blackness was beginning to fade out of the storm, day was breaking, and they glimpsed alongside a cluster of jackies toiling in flooding seas at hawsers lashed round two great turret guns. More than ever convinced by this escape that his eyes were needed on the bridge, Captain Kendrick stayed steadfast in his purpose. The two officers felt awe as they looked at him, that he should have sensed, where their eyes could not see, the danger they had shaved by a hair's breadth. Sometimes now his head fell forward, but the hand on the indicator lever was ever nervously alive to feel the ship and the raving seas, and he was snatching her from death, inch by inch and hour by hour.

## V

In the early hours of the storm, Arthur Valentine was battering like a shuttle-cock between the sides of his berth, sicker in mind than in body, for manifold terrors had come to prey upon him. Without confidence in the captain of the ship, he felt that his own cowardice was responsible for failure to act when the issue had been almost within his grasp. Through the dragging hours, as the ship cried aloud in every racking beam and rivet, or quaked as if her rearing bows had rammed a rock, Valentine convinced himself that the captain would not have dared refuse him if he had faced it out and insisted that the first officer take command.

"Don't I own the steamer?" he groaned. "Can't a man do what he pleases with his own property? And I let myself be bluffed out like a whipped pup. Only a lunatic would have defied me. Of course he's tucked away in a corner trying to pray down a storm like this. What did Carr tell me? What did Parlin say?"

On the heels of these emotions came the dreadful instant when the *Suwannee* took aboard the sea that swept her bridge. Valentine was flung out of his berth to the floor in a bruised heap, and heard the crash of glass and the riot of water which tumbled solid into the saloon outside his room. Before he could get footing his room was awash, and floating luggage knocked him this way and that. He crawled outside and collided with a half-clad man who was wringing his hands as he wailed:

"Save yourself. We're sinking. Look at the whole Atlantic Ocean in here."

"What's the matter? What's happened?" gasped Valentine.

"What's happened? I heard the captain had killed the first officer, or strung him up, or something awful. And now there surely is hell to pay. Why don't somebody come to our rescue?"

What passed with him for duty, even the high tide of heroic impulse in his whole life, impelled Valentine to struggle up the stairway to the "social hall" on the deck above. He believed that the risk of being washed overboard was very great, he was almost certain the crazy captain would knock him down or shoot him, but he was braced ready to meet these things. It was a desperate situation demanding a desperate remedy. He felt vague admiration and pity for himself, as he made ready for the plunge on deck. But a dripping sailor barred the way.

"I'm willing to run the risk," protested the hero. "It's my duty to save the ship. She belongs to me."

"So does Cape Horn an' the Statue of Liberty," returned the seaman soothingly. "But you don't want to play with 'em now. They'll keep all right. Nobody goes on deck. Them's orders. Just sit down an' play you're a train of cars. It's lots of fun, an' it's safe an' dry."

Valentine tried to pass him and was thrust back so violently that he fell upon a comatose passenger stretched on a set-tee. This victim sputtered feeble protest and other voices were raised. Valentine noticed now that several men and women were huddled in this corner of the deck-house, fled from the desolation below stairs. One of them screamed above the clamor of the wind:

"The ship is all smashed to pieces and nobody knows what to do next."

"I am going to get forward somehow, and put the first officer in command, if he's alive," cried Valentine. "It's life or death for all of us, and my word must go. Doesn't this fool sailor know who I am?"

Alas, these shivering refugees scented a new alarm. The poor young man had gone mad with fright, and they, too, tried to soothe him, while a woman of them sobbingly implored the sailor to take him away before he became violent. Valentine cursed them all, and clawed his way down the hand-rail to the saloon to seek some other exit. The way forward was blocked by savage men dragging tarpaulins, and they kicked him out of their path when he would argue with them. He splashed back and forth, like a rat in a trap, falling against bulk-heads and furniture, or pitched clear off his feet, until, worn out, he slunk back in sullen silence up among the little company in the deck-house who waited for they knew not what.

So much of Valentine's purpose had been hammered out of him that nausea resumed its sway, and he clung to a cushion, helpless through interminable hours. When he was able to pull himself together and make feeble effort, it seemed as if the pitching of the steamer were less terrifying, and through an after-port the daylight gleamed. He dragged himself to it, and caught a glimpse of somber sea and sky. The blizzard had passed.

Then strong hands were thumping on the outer door, and a steward tugged at the inside fastenings. In a flurry of spray three burden-bearers staggered into the room, between them a great limp bulk in oil-skins, whose face was hidden by a sou'wester. As the seamen paused to veer ever so gently around the corner of the hallway, Valentine went close to the third officer who led the way, and said with a novel timidity in his voice:

"I am Mr. Valentine, owner of the line. Can you tell me what has happened, please?"

"It's the skipper—frozen up, busted up, dyin' it looks to me, sir," was the husky response. "He's brought her through the blow lone-handed. I never seen another man afloat as could ha' done the trick he did."

The young man trailed after the stumbling procession which turned into a large stateroom aft. Before swift hands had removed the boots and outer garments, a physician from among the passengers was busy with hot water and bandages. The Irish stewardess was weeping as she tried to help. They paid no heed to Valentine, who returned to the doorway as often as he was jostled to one side.

The three seamen huddled in the passage talked softly among themselves, and Valentine heard:

"I tink he give der first mate vat vas comin' to him, eh? Und if der skipper's room vas flooded out, den Mister Parlin must been sloshin' round mit der door gelocked, most drownded. Goot enough."

"It's sure all right if the old man done it. An' him with two bum legs to start with, buckin' her through last night. Him gettin' smashed galley-west, rudder busted—Hell's Delight! what a mess! He looked as if he was all in when we pried him loose from them slings that was holdin' him up."

"Ask the doc if he can pull him through, will you?"

Valentine tiptoed in, as the doctor whispered with a warning gesture:

"I think so. His head needs a good many stitches, and there is an ankle to set and some ribs to mend. But he will take a lot of killing yet. Come, men, you must clear out of the hall. He will be coming to presently."

What Valentine heard was mightily reinforced by that which he saw with eyes that were misty and troubled. Before him lay such grim reality of duty done as the shallows of his life had never touched. Groping in a welter of new thoughts, he made his way to the deck and went forward as far as he dared, amazed at sight of the havoc wrought overnight. Perched on his wrecked bridge the figure of Peter Carr swung against the brightening sky. He had learned who Valentine was, and called down:

"We'll work her up to Sandy Hook without any blisterin' salvage bills, sir. There's a few of us left."

"And these are the kind of men I was going to stand on their heads," said Valentine to himself, as he clambered up and asked many eager questions. Nor was Peter Carr at all backward in painting with vivid word and gesture the story of the night, down to a parting shaft of crafty comment:

"And there's them that thinks the old man is a softy an' ought to be knittin' tidies in a home for derelict seafarin' men."

Restlessly seeking the captain's stateroom again and again, Valentine was denied admittance until late in the afternoon. When the doctor let him in, the old man opened his eyes and his weather-scarred face lightened with a kindly gleam of recognition. Valentine flushed and began hurried speech:

"I hope you'll forget that letter.... Is there anything I can do?... If you want to go to sea again, or if you don't, or whatever else———"

The doctor raised a silencing finger. Valentine bent over to stroke a bandaged hand which moved on the blanket just enough to pat his with a little parental caress. The doctor nudged Valentine to withdraw, as the captain whispered drowsily:

"All-l's well.... You didn't know any better, did you?... So He bringeth them into their desired haven."

*"You are a disgrace to Yale, all of you."*

# A VICTORY UNFORESEEN

"That's enough for to-night. Turn around and go home. You are a disgrace to Yale, all of you, and you're the worst of a bad lot, Number Five."

The Head Coach roared his convictions through a megaphone from the bow of the panting launch, and the coxswain caught up the words and flung them in piping echoes at the heads of the eight sullen oarsmen facing him. The grind of the slides and the tearing swash of blades abruptly ceased as the slim shell trailed with dying headway to the skitter of the resting oars. Backs burned dull red by the sun of long June days drooped in relaxation that was not all weariness. John Hastings, at Number Five, remembered when to slip along the shore; heading homeward in the twilight after pulling four miles over the New London course, was the keenest joy he had ever known. Now, with the Harvard race less than a week away, the daily toil was a nightmare of ineffective striving. The pulsating shell hesitated between strokes, it rolled without visible cause, and seemed sentiently to realize that the crew was rowing as eight men, not as one.

The boat circled wide and the men swept it listlessly toward the lights of the Quarters at Gales Ferry. They had just undergone the severest ordeal in all athletic training in their race against the stop watch, yet if the work had been good they would have finished vibrant as steel springs, spurting in this welcome home stretch like the sweep of a hawk. Squatted on the boathouse float a little later, dousing pails of water over his sweating shoulders, Hastings heard the Stroke growl to Number Seven:

"What's the matter with you loafers back there?"

"I'm not behind," retorted Seven, with hair-trigger irritability. "The trouble is in the middle of the boat. Hastings is too heavy to row in form this year, and he seems to have gone to pieces in the last month. That's where the worst break in the swing comes. Did you hear the Old Man threaten to take him out of the boat and get him a job as a farm hand?"

The Culprit wearily picked himself up and dressed in a dark corner of the boathouse, shunning conversation. After the training-table supper, the Head Coach and his younger staff of graduate experts, who had flocked back to help stem the adverse tide, summoned the crew into the parlor of the lonely old farmhouse. The Nestor of Yale rowing, who for twenty years had taught Yale crews how to win, leaned against the battered piano and looked at the ruddy and wholesome young faces around him. It might have been a council about to weigh matters of life and death, so grave was the troubled aspect of the waiting group, so stern the set of their leader's bulldog jaw.

To-night he had something of their nervous uncertainty, and it showed in the way his strong fingers played with the fringe of the faded piano cover. Picking up the well-worn log-book in which was recorded year by year the daily work of Yale crews from January to July, he turned the leaves until a text was found. Then, slamming the book on the piano with a vigor that made the aged wires complain, he said:

"The work has been discouraging ever since you came to New London, but to-day it was so bad that it made me sick. I never saw faster conditions on this course, and yet you clawed your way up river in twenty-two minutes and ten seconds. That is nearly a quarter of a mile slower than last year's crew. Do you know what this means? You are strong enough; you have had plenty of coaching, and I intend to work the very souls out of you to-morrow. If there is no improvement—well, you had better jump overboard and drown yourself after the race than to go back to New Haven. No man's place is safe in this crew, even if the race is only four days off. This means you, Number Five."

There were no songs around the piano, as was the custom in happier evenings, nor did the Head Coach pound the tinkling yellow keys and lead the chorus of "Jolly Boating Weather," as he had done so many nights of so many years when the work had been satisfactory. At nine o'clock the Captain called out gruffly:

"All out for the walk, fellows."

The squad filed through the gate into the darkness of the country lane for the end of the day's routine, with John Hastings trailing in rear of the procession. He had become fond of this nightly ramble, feeling on terms of intimacy with every stone wall, low-roofed farmhouse and fragrant orchard, and courting the smell of the lush June country side as the rarest of sleeping potions. But to-night he strode with head down, turning over and over in his mind the haunting list of his sins as an oarsman. Always with him of late, they had been driven home anew by the events of recent hours. He looked up at the quiet sea of little stars, and his self-reproach unconsciously changed to the form of a prayer:

"O Lord, help me to get my power on, and to keep my slide under me. I never worked half so hard, but I know I am heavier and slower than I used to be. Help me to stay on the crew. I don't ask it for my sake, but—but Mother's coming to the race, and this is my third year on the crew, and she never saw a race, and if I'm kicked off now it will break her heart. It means so much to her, and I am all she has. And—and there's Cynthia Wells—she's coming, too. Oh, it means everything to me, everything."

Such a man was he in the glory of his superbly conditioned strength, such a boy in the narrow limits of his life's horizon, bounded in this crisis by the Quarters, the boathouse, the crew, and the shining stretch of river!

The next morning sparkled with a cool breeze from the Sound, and its salty tang was a tonic after the sultry days that had tugged at the weights of all the men, except Hastings, until they were almost gaunt. When the crew was boated for the forenoon practice, the exhortations of the Head Coach were even hopeful. But after he had sent them on the first stretch at full speed, even the *blasé* old engineer of the launch could see that things were going wrong in the same old way. The emotions of the Head Coach were too large for words and with sinister patience he made them row another spurt. Before he could begin to speak, Hastings knew that there was still a break in the swing at Number Five, and the confirmation came in almost a tone of entreaty from the launch:

"You are still behind, Number Five, while the rest of the crew is swinging better. Try, for Heaven's sake, to get your shoulders on it, and swing them up to the perpendicular as if the devil were after you. Do you want seven other men to pull your hundred and ninety pounds of beef and muscle like so much freight in the boat? I have told you these things a thousand times, and you must hang on to them this time, or I can't risk bothering with you any more. All ready, coxswain, steer for that red barn across the river."

"Forward all. G-e-t ready. R-o-w-w!" shrieked the coxswain.

Within the first thirty strokes Hastings felt that he was rowing in no better form than before, although never had he been so grimly determined to row better. Stung to the soul by the taunt of the coach, he threw his splendid shoulders against the twelve-foot sweep, striving always to be a little ahead of Number Six, whose instant of catch was signaled by the tell-tale tightening of the crease in the back of his neck. The Captain called:

"Give her ten good ones, and look out for the stroke. It's going up."

"O-n-e, T-w-o, Thr-e-e, F-o-u-r, F-i-v-e," gasped the eight, in husky chorus to the cadence of the catch.

"Slo-w down on your y-o-u-r slides," yelled the bobbing coxswain. "You're be-h-i-n-d, Number Five."

Hastings could have throttled the coxswain for this. He had heard it so often that it cut him on the raw. The Head Coach picked up the damnable refrain:

"You are behind, Number Five."

Recalling how once, to fill an idle half hour, he had enumerated sixty-four faults possible in rowing a single stroke, Hastings was sure that in this spurt he was committing all these and several as yet unrecorded. The futility of his flurried effort became maddening. Where was his strength going?

The verdict befell as the launch steamed alongside, and a substitute perched on the cabin roof jumped to the deck at the beckoning of the Head Coach, who said, with a ring of sincere regret:

"I am afraid I'll have to try a change at Number Five, to see whether we can patch up that break. Get in there, Matthews. Better get out and take a rest, Hastings."

The cast-off crawled aboard the launch and went aft to the cock-pit under the awnings, where he could be alone. Holding himself bravely under the sympathetic eyes of his comrades, he watched the substitute grip the oar, still warm from his own calloused hands. Nor did he yet realize what had befallen him, and felt vague relief that the struggle was done. At dinner he was cheerful and flippant and the other oarsmen admired his "sand."

The reality began to overtake him when he went to his room under the eaves, and anxiously asked the Stroke:

"Well, how did you go it with a new Number Five?"

"A little better," replied his room-mate, with evident reluctance. "The Old Man says he is going to keep Matthews in your seat for the race. It's a hard thing to talk about, Jack. You know how broken up we all feel about it, don't you? We know you tried your level best, and your extra weight this year made you slow, and you couldn't help that. Heard from your folks lately?"

Hastings was reminded of things he had feared to let rush into the foreground. He had been too preoccupied to think of looking for mail downstairs, and was starting for the door, when the Stroke halted him with:

"Oh, I forgot to tell you I brought up a couple of letters for you. There they are, on the bureau."

Hastings recognized his mother's handwriting on one envelope, that of Cynthia Wells on the other. He appeared to hesitate which of them to open first, and in this hour of trial, his choice was swayed by an impulse as old as the world:

The letter which he preferred was dated on board the yacht *Diana*, off New Haven, and he read slowly to himself:

DEAR OLD JACK:

I am so happy to be almost at the scene of your victories, past and to come. And to think I have never seen you row! How foolish and inconsiderate of Father to drag me abroad so early two seasons on end. But I am bringing all the heaped-up enthusiasm of three years— think of that! I suppose you are as calm as *blanc mange*, while I am jabbering rowing at everybody in sight, and am getting really awfully clever about strokes and catches (are they so very catching?). Your classmate, Dickie Munson, is on board, and has been coaching me up on the technical mysteries, and spinning many jolly yarns about you. I hear you are to be elected captain of next year's crew, the very grandest honor at Yale. May I offer congratulations in advance? I do so want to see you, and will be one of the worshipping admirers of your prowess! Of course you will be busy until after the race, and then you are to come down to the *Diana* as soon as ever you can. Don't forget that I will have an eye on you all the way down the course.

   Yours as ever,

                    Cynthia.

Hastings tucked this letter in an inside pocket with reverent care, and without speaking, sought next what his mother would say:

MY DEAREST BOY:

I have decided to come North by sea, and will sail on the *Mohican* to-morrow. The fare is considerably less than by rail, and as you have insisted upon paying the expenses of my wonderful trip, I want to save you all I can. The ship is due at New York late in the afternoon of the twenty-seventh, the day before the race, and I plan to take the earliest train to New London, to reach there that night, if possible. I have the address of the boarding house in which you have reserved the nice room for me, and you will not have to worry at all about having me met, as, of course, you will not be able to come down from the Quarters. It will be hard to bear, this being so near you on that last night, unable even to kiss you good night and God bless you. After the race you can come to my room, and we will go to New Haven on the special train with the crew. Of course you are going to win again, when your mother is coming all the way from the South to see her boy fight for old Yale. Oh, I want so much to see my big, handsome boy, and it will be music for me to hear the thousands cheering him. I received the ticket for the observation train in Car

Fifteen, and I can find it at the station, as you directed me, so don't have me on your mind for a moment. I pray for you each night, and may God bring me safe to you.

Your loving and adoring

LITTLE MOTHER.

"I don't see how I can let her know," observed Hastings with a long sigh.

"Which?" asked the Stroke, as he searched his comrade's face with shrewd kindliness.

"I mean Mother, of course," was the reply, followed by a sharp prick of conscience. "She is coming up by sea, she is on the way now. The other letter was from a—from a friend. She is to be here, too."

"You ought to meet her in New York—your mother, of course. She is first in your thoughts, I am sure," advised the Stroke, with a perceptible shade of disbelief. "Just let her see that you are sound and lusty, that's what she will care most about. She will be sorry for your sake, not for her own."

Throwing himself across his cot, Hastings looked out of the nearest window, down the river to where the flag above the Harvard Quarters slashed the sky like a ribbon of flame. There were the enemy whom he had helped to defeat, and now it seemed an honorable thing, greatly to be desired, even to row on a beaten crew. The tousled head went to the pillow, and he could no longer help pouring out his heart to his friend:

"Nothing can make it any worse than it is. I have worked every summer so far, and I was going to have a real vacation this year, the first since I have been in college. Now I can't bear to think of any good times, with disgrace hanging over me. I am going to apply for my summer job again, but I've been working in the office of a Yale man, and I am afraid he won't want to have a slob around him who was kicked off the crew four days before the race, will he? Of course he won't. The last month has been simply hell. Mother has been living in the thought of this trip just to see me row against Harvard, and—and there is a girl—well, I am a big, whining, useless baby, that's all."

The Stroke was an older man by five years, who had known a man's stress and sorrows before his college days began. Had he been a man of readier speech, he would have tried somehow to make the sorrowing boy realize that there were other worlds to conquer, wider and more inspiring fields in the years beyond. Yet there was something quite fine in this absorption in the crew; it was what one ought to feel at twenty-one, and it might be better for him to fight it out alone. The Stroke was glad when the youngster marched out of the room without more words. "I hope he stands the gaff," thought the elder man.

Hastings' first impulse had been to flee the place, and he was still busy with the longing to be anywhere away from the sights and sounds that racked him because they were so infinitely much to him. While he struggled with the decision, the eight began to make ready for the long afternoon practice. As the shell swung out of sight around the curve of the shore, Hastings had not believed it possible that any one could feel as lonely and neglected as he at that moment. Just then he saw a University substitute standing idly in the boathouse door, and he remembered that with one transferred to the eight, and another laid off with a cold, this youngster, Bates, was the sole survivor of the trio which had its own thankless duties and burdens. The intending fugitive made a choice then and there, as he slid down the bank, shouting:

"Aren't you going out to-day to keep tabs on the Red-Heads?"

The solitary substitute ruefully shook his head:

"No, I haven't any one to man the pair-oar with me, and I'm no good in a single shell. And I ought to be over at the start right now, for the tip is out that Harvard is going to try the four miles on time, their last attempt. How am I going to catch their time, I want to know, with nobody to help me?"

Hastings laid hold of the bow of the pair-oared boat as he said:

"Get hold of the other end of the tub, and we'll put her in the water. I might as well be a substitute, too, if there is work for me to do. We'll hold the watch on the Johnny Harvards in great shape."

The substitute glimpsed something of the sacrifice and struggle in Hastings' offer to help him, but he could not know it all, because he was only a "sub." The two were bending over their stretchers lacing the shoes, when the launch slipped past the float so quietly that the substitutes did not hear it. The Head Coach, however, standing on the forward deck, heard Hastings say to his mate with an evident effort:

"I came pretty near playing the baby act and running away, but if I can help the Yale shell to go faster by being out of it, I am glad of it. That's what I am rowing for, anyhow. And if I can be of any use as a substitute, why, that's what I am here for, too. It is all for Yale, isn't it?"

The two in the pair-oar rowed across the river, landed a half mile above the start of the four-mile course, and walked down the railroad track.

"We can't do anything more than catch their time over the first mile," observed the experienced Bates; "but that will give us a good line on the gait they are going." Hastings meekly followed instructions to hurry to the hill opposite the first-mile flag, and be ready to wave his handkerchief when the Harvard crew should pass him. Bates, at the start with a stop watch, would snap the time at this signal. In dust and quivering heat, Hastings trudged along the ties, crept up the hill and lay on his stomach under a tree, waiting the appearance of the Harvard crew. The tears could not be held back at thought of this humiliation, of the abysmal gap between this petty spying in ambush, and all the days in which he had swung by this first-mile flag in the University eight.

There was much time for meditation, and while the first shock had wrecked his every hope, he began to patch the fabric of his dearest dream, until he was ready to believe that, even more clearly than his mother, Cynthia Wells would understand. She would see that he had tried to do his best, that the failure was blackened by nothing left undone, and that his great disappointment was of a piece with those troubles which knit closer the bonds of friendship. She would know that it was "all for Yale," that winning the race was more important than anything else in the world, and he ached for the words of comfort and inspiration she would be so eager to offer. If friendship meant anything it meant help in such times as this.

## II

On the day before the race Hastings' occupation as a substitute was gone. The shadow of the morrow was over the Quarters, the atmosphere was funereal, and the strapping oarsmen were coddled like infants. He had no part in the excitement, and was free to meet his mother in New York that afternoon. The news he must bear her made him as nervous as if he were facing the tussle of the eights. After farewells with his other comrades he sought the Stroke, who grasped the hand of the sorrowful exile in a crushing grip.

"Keep your nerve, Jack," said he; "it will all come out in the wash. I know there's a girl in it, and if she is the right sort, she will understand."

Hastings flushed at mention of the feminine factor, as he stammered:

"Of course she will understand. She is that kind, all right. But I hope to Heaven I'll never clap eyes on Gales Ferry again. Damn the place! Goodbye. You've been a brick to me, and lots of comfort."

After he had gone, the Stroke looked up from his book for some time, while a tender smile softened his strong mouth. He had found a girl who could understand, and he hoped the same good fortune for his friend.

When the train passed through New Haven, Hastings wore a hang-dog air, fearing recognition. A runaway from New London the day before the race, his college town was the last place on earth in which he wished to be seen.

As he neared New York he braced himself for the meeting with his mother, blindly fearing that she would be sorely disappointed in him. But the *Mohican* had been delayed by heavy weather along the coast and a smothering fog off Sandy Hook, and could not be expected to reach her dock before seven o'clock of the following morning.

Hastings felt as if he were cast away on a desert island. He yearned for his mother now, but she was somewhere out in the fog, and he was alone in New York, alone through the long night before the race, with all its smarting, thrilling memories. Long after midnight, unable to coax drowsiness, his thoughts went homing back to the Quarters as he knew the place in these last hours.

He could hear the call of the robin at daybreak in the tree by his window, the call that had aroused him to face the issues of two races when he was Number Five. He could picture the morning scenes, the hush of lawn and house, the enforced lounging on bed and sofa until the summons to be ready and dressed at the boathouse.

Then he recalled the tense waiting on the float for the call of the whistle of the referee's yacht, how the year before they had sat together in the sunshine and sung the chorus of "Jolly Boating Weather." Since then it had become to him a battle song, a chant profoundly burdened with sentiment and solemnity. He could not hear it without feeling a lump in his breast. Now the shell would be launched, the men seating themselves with unusual care, and the coaches would shake hands from stroke to bow as the eight shoved off to row over to the start.... He wiped the sweat from his face and came back to the stifling room of the hotel in New York, and the sense of cruel isolation.

It was almost daylight when Hastings fell asleep, more tired than he knew, and when he awoke, a glance at his watch told him that he had overslept, and that it was nearly ten o'clock. The reply to a frantic telephone message was that all the passengers of the *Mohican* had gone ashore shortly after eight o'clock. His mother had gone to New London without him, and the express train into which he dove was due to arrive at the scene of conflict barely in time to connect with the observation train, if all conditions favored. Ten minutes behind time, he was running through the New London station, as the tail of the rearward observation cars was vanishing around a curve of the track yard, with cheering in its wake.

Vainly pursuing on foot, Hastings came to a standstill, stranded and alone, unable even to see the race, about to start five miles up the river. Walking down to the nearest wharf, he could see through the arches of the great railroad bridge the festooned yachts stretching in squadrons beyond, and between them only a little patch of silver lane where the crews would finish.

## III

Shortly after noon, there stepped from the first "special" into New London a fragile yet sprightly little woman in rustling black, alone, but confident and unafraid. Her sweet face was made beautiful, even youthful, by the flush of excitement that tinted her cheek so delicately beneath her silvered hair. Violets were pinned at her waist; in one hand she carried a flag of Yale blue, and in the other a decorative souvenir programme "containing the pictures of all the crews." Those near her in the car had watched with pleasure her vivacious interest in this booklet, but only the gentleman sitting next her had been taken into her confidence. Thirty years out of college, he was come from the far West to his class reunion, and he, too, had a boy in Yale. Fortunately or otherwise, he had not kept in touch with the most recent news of the heroic figures of aquatics, and he knew not even the names of the crew of the year at Yale, so that she could enlighten his lamentable ignorance and right willingly. The "souvenir" booklet had been printed a week before the race, too soon to record the change in the *personnel* of the Yale eight, and there was her boy's picture filling a page, a massive young giant, most scantily clothed. The man from the West saw in the picture the mother's brown eyes, and his heart was stirred, for he knew what it was to have an only son with his mother's eyes.

"Yes, John has been on the crew three years," she confided, "and he will be the captain next year. I fairly live with him in spirit through the whole six months of the training season. He has had a very hard time this season, and lately his letters have been a little despondent. But I was never so delighted as when I learned from the head-lines of this morning's newspapers that there has been a wonderful improvement in the last week. Oh, I am excited, there is no use trying to deny it. It is almost too big an event for an old woman to survive."

The gray-haired stranger was comforting, and in the recesses of his memory found certain eulogies pronounced by his son regarding "Jack Hastings, the biggest man in his class, by Jove!" He insisted upon presenting two of his own classmates, and they bowed low in formal tribute to the "mother of the next captain of the crew."

The porter must leave her bag in the station, for she could not wait to go to the boarding house when the air was full of tingling sights and sounds, all the excitement and flaunting color paying homage to the prowess of John Hastings. She found Car Fifteen, and sat in a beautiful dream, watching the holiday crowds fill the canopied lengths of open train. What a tale to tell when she should come again to the little colorless village in the South! It seemed impossible to drink it all in when the train began to move and in a few moments the amazing panorama of the Thames flashed into view. The eager eyes of the oarsman's mother passed quickly over the gorgeous marine pictures, by the twisting length of the riotous train, up, up the river toward the quiet reaches, hoping to discern the white house on the high bank and the big blue flag floating above the Quarters at Gales Ferry, a scene she knew from many descriptions.

Soon the train had passed the yachts and the crowds massed on shore, and was opposite the red-roofed home of the Harvard crew, whose crimson flag seemed to her to flaunt an insolent defiance. In near-by cars fluttered many Harvard flags, as the partisans from Cambridge chanted their slogan, inspired by the sight of their rowing camp across the river. She turned to look at the offenders with reproof in her manner. How could they be so misguided as to cheer for Harvard? How dreadful it was to think that if John should be beaten, every one of them would be shouting even louder for joy. So she turned to gaze at the Yale Quarters, which she could see quite plainly, and the ugly brown boathouse squatted at the water's edge.

Her color came and went, and stayed in a brilliant patch when she saw, with a quick intake of breath, a yellow streak appear in front of the boathouse and a number of Lilliputians walking beside it. There seemed an eternity of delay before the wisp of a shell settled on the water, and nine figures climbed into it, while her heart was tripping furiously.

The thing became in motion, it was crawling across the river like a mechanical toy, with frequent pauses. Could this be the Crew, this fragile thing that moved over the water so slowly? A roar from the Harvard cars, and Mrs. Hastings turned to see a similar set of manikins swaying in as absurd a boat, heading out from "Red Top." The mother looked at them only for an instant, because the Yale crew was crossing the river faster than she could realize, and soon it was half a mile above the start, paddling and drifting down with the tide to get into position at its stake-boat. She wanted to call imploringly to the referee to bring the crew nearer, nearer, so that she might see the men, and count from the bow, to two, three, four, *five*. Presently the shell swung round, parallel with the shore, and maneuvered into position scarcely twenty yards from the observation train hanging on the edge of the bank.

At last the mother could look for Number Five. She counted with an eager and quivering finger. No, she must have made a mistake—that was not John at Number Five. They must have shifted him to another seat at the last moment.

She flung away all method and searched the stern young faces from stroke to bow, from bow to stroke and back again, with yearning agony of intensity. She made bold to ask that the gentleman next her lend her his field-glasses for a moment, and focused them on the shell, seeking in vain. The color had fled from her cheeks, and she sat back, white and silent, beyond speech. Around her raved the cheers of thousands, but the rocketing "rahs" for Yale sounded in her ears like some barbaric funeral chant. She had become old and weak far beyond her years.

Her distress was unnoticed, and through a haze she saw the long shells leap from their leashes with incredible suddenness in tearing cascades of foam. To the mourning mother the race was no more than an exhibition of automatons, as Harvard took the lead, and then the long Yale swing cut it down remorselessly, foot by foot, until the gap was closed. She closed her eyes with a weary sigh, but rallied in a little while to try to make herself heard above the din. Yale was spurting gallantly, and those around her were oblivious to the quavering voice and its vital questions:

"Where is John Hastings? Number Five in the Yale Crew? Where has he gone? What have they done with him? Oh, tell me, tell me, tell me, please. I am his mother."

Yale hopes drooped as Harvard met the spurt, and in the lull a young man of a kindly face saw that she was ill, and leaned toward her to ask whether he could help. She was able to make him understand, and there was a huskiness in his voice that came not all from cheering, as he said:

"Why, he's all right, safe and sound as a dollar. He was taken out of the boat four or five days ago, and Matthews put in his place. No, I don't know what the matter was. Too heavy, I fancy. I'm awfully sorry for you."

*Jack Hasting's mother cannot find her boy in the crew.*

Where else should a boy flee in time of trouble than straight to his mother's arms? Therefore the reason for his disappearance must be an alarming one. Then she felt a blaze of swift anger. It was an outrageous act of injustice, this deed of the Yale coaches. They were no better than conspirators thus to treat the best oarsman they had. It was not in a mother's philosophy to grasp the view-point that what was best for Yale was best for all who fought for its glory. She vowed that a reckoning was due, and that her duty was to see these coaches, and tell them the truth before she left the scene. And so, between wrath and tears, she saw the race end, saw the Yale crew sweep across the finish line, victors over Harvard by four lengths. This was what she had come to see, what she had lived in the hope of seeing through three long years, and now all had turned to ashes.

Wearily she threaded a way through the thronging railroad station, found a cab and gave the driver directions for reaching the boarding house where a room awaited her. Her steps faltered as she toiled up the stairs, and all that gave her strength for the ascent was the flicker of hope that John might be there, or that some message had come from him. The room was empty, the table bare of letter or telegram. Carefully laying her bonnet and jacket on a chair, she looked at her face in a mirror, and it frightened her. Although she was eager to be out again in search of the way to Gales Ferry, rest was imperative, and she crossed over to the bed and lay down for a few moments until the dizzy faintness should pass.

## IV

When John Hastings drifted down to the wharf nearest the railroad station, he laid an almost aimless course. While he could not see the race, he was drawn to the harbor into which flowed the river, the river by whose bank, five miles away, his comrades were waiting for the summons, and perhaps even then singing "Jolly Boating Weather," as it was never sung at any other time.

Through the maze of fragile shipping flying the flags of a dozen yacht clubs threaded a naphtha launch hurrying toward the bridge, the cock-pit gay with white gowns and blue uniforms, and Yale colors fluttering at bow and stern. The outcast bestowed no more than a scowling glance on the glittering, humming pleasure craft, and was about to saunter shoreward with a vague intent of hovering near the telegraph office until the result of the race should be known, when the beckoning flurry of several handkerchiefs delayed his retreat.

He walked to the end of the wharf in idlest curiosity, and the possibility staggered him only an instant before he knew the fact. There was no mistaking the trim and jaunty figure in the bow for any one else than Cynthia Wells herself, as she flicked the steering wheel over and ran the craft close to the stringpiece, while the sailor in the stern held fast with a boat hook. Her voice was lifted in peremptory command:

"Scramble right down here this minute, and tumble aboard, Jack. We are awfully late already. Broke down on the way from the *Diana*. I don't know what in the world you are doing here, but we can't pass such an image of desolation. Hurry, please. I am the skipper to-day."

Jack would have vastly preferred to run away. This meeting was not at all what he had planned. His misery loved company limited to one, and that one was hedged about by half a dozen laughing men and girls out for a holiday lark. He realized how sorry a figure of a man he was in this scene, but retreat meant cowardly flight, and there was the shadow of consolation in being near her. The grip of "Dickie" Munson's hand spelled understanding of the situation as the classmate said:

"We're tickled to death to kidnap you this way, Jack. It's a tough day for you, I know, but you must not miss the race. Get forward. There's room by Miss Wells, and, of course, she is dying to see you."

When he found himself standing by the side of Cynthia, she was alert and absorbed in steering the launch with confident ease toward the swirling channel between the arches of the bridge, where small craft darted and drifted in common eagerness to find positions along the last mile of the swarming course.

The jolly wind whipped a straying lock of gold-shot hair across her eyes, and she brushed it aside with an impatient gesture. Her adorable face, warm with the glow of many summer days of sun and breeze, was set in serious alertness. Standing straight and tall, head thrown back and shoulders squared, the poise and look of her were as athletic as the bearing of the man at her side. With her mind wholly intent on the business in hand, she said crisply:

"I have the right of way over that tub to port. Why doesn't he head inshore? How is the tide through that middle arch, Jack? You ought to know."

He made brief reply. Unreasonably sensitive, he did not realize that her preoccupation was essential. At the least, he had expected she would speak some ready word of the sympathy he craved, because he stood for a tragedy in which she ought to show concern. Did she not know, could she not feel what this flight up the course meant to him, "Jack Hastings, Number Five"? But the girl at the wheel was too busy even to note the gloom in his face, as she shot the launch into a roomy berth near the three and a half mile flag, at the edge of the streak of open water. Then Cynthia turned to Hastings, held out a firm brown hand, and said with a happy smile:

"There, congratulate me. Could your coxswain, with his absurd little megaphone and all his importance, do a neater trick of steering than that? Now, you poor unfortunate boy, I am ready to hear all about your troubles. We heard yesterday, when we came ashore at New London, that you had been evicted, or had gone on strike, or something of the sort. Are you all broken up over it, and how did it happen? I am terribly disappointed, too. I came on to see you win a race. I don't care a rap for the other heroes. Poor old Jack! He looks as if he were chief mourner."

She patted his hand with a motherly air, and the mourner sighed heavily. Evidently she was making a gallant effort to hide her genuine emotion from the alien company. He tried to imitate her lightness of manner as he replied, with a laugh that was a trifle shaky:

"Yes, I have been out of the crew four days, Cynthia, and it seems four years. It was awfully good of you to pick me up, but I don't know whether I am glad or not. Perhaps you ought to have left me alone."

"And why, Mister Knight of the Sorrowful Countenance? Didn't you want to see me?"

There was archness in the query, even a trace of pretty coquetry in her air. Where was the kinship of souls, that wonderful symphony of understanding he had dreamed of as come true? With a fierce onset of earnestness, he confided:

"I wanted to see you more than any one else in the world. I wanted to see you more than I wanted to see my mother. She is looking for me now. She is on that train up yonder. It has been a pretty hard day for me, and I thought it would be for you."

She tried to make amends:

"Why, of course, it is a dreadful disappointment for you, and for me, and for all your friends, Jack. But aren't you glad it gave you the chance to be here? I certainly am. And I'm trying to make the best of it, and so must you. You are the same old Jack, you know, in the crew or out."

The first smile in days broke over his face. If he was the same old Jack to her, the rest of the world could go hang. He was about to tell her what he ached to reveal in a rush of pent-up desire, what the Crew stood for, and how much of his life was bound up in it. She caught the kindling light in his face, and before he spoke, she thought this light was all for her. That his interest should be absorbed in the crew, rather than in Miss Cynthia Wells, piqued her, even now, as he began:

"I was afraid the crash was coming for some time. Nobody can know how I hoped and worried through those weeks, when I felt that I was slipping back. I did not write you about it, because I could not believe there was any serious danger of my being thrown out at the last moment, and I knew it would harrow you to share this worry with me. I—I—wanted your——"

The classmate behind him jumped to his feet and shouted:

"There they come! Yale! Yale! Yale!"

Hastings glanced along the water level up-river. Two black dots were visible, each fluttering thread-like tentacles. Abreast of them trailed the observation train, like a huge serpent of gaudy hues. He bit his lip and trembled with sudden excitement, while Cynthia Wells stood, one hand shading her eyes, so eagerly intent that it was plain that she had forgotten the oarsman out of the shell. The sea of blue, rippling along the train, told him that Yale was leading. He shut his eyes, fearing, until it sickened him, that some accident might happen to Yale, even with what seemed to be a safe lead.

## V

To those who did not know, the winners seemed to be playing with rowing as they swept toward the finish. With no apparent effort the blue-tipped blades flashed in and out, without even a feather of spray. Forward and back again rocked eight bare backs, working as if coupled on the same connecting rod. Hands slipped easily into arched and heaving chests, and shot out with lightning speed; slow, slower, swooped the shoulders squared beneath necks like fluted columns and heads poised with airy grace. As Hastings leaned far out on the bow of the launch, waving his hat in a fury of approval, the shell rushed by him not twenty feet away, and the complaining roar of the slides was music in his ears. He could feel with that agony of effort to keep in form when every muscle cried out in rebellion, and the choking fight for breath, and yet, with it all, the glory of making the swing and catch fairly lift the quivering shell. And he knew, also, the intoxication of the sight of the Harvard crew laboring astern, as seen through eyes half blinded with sweat.

Hastings was lifted out of himself until he saw his crew cease rowing and the oars trail like the wings of a tired bird. Then the defeated crew went past him. There were breaks in the swing, heads nodded on the catch, backs were bending, and bodies swaying athwartships. It was anything now to cross the line and rest.

Hastings had a new realization of what these whipped oarsmen felt, they whose high hopes were wrecked, whose labor, as long and as faithful as that of the winners, had gone for nought. After all, he did not belong with the winners, he was one of the losers, and he wished he might shake their hands. He cheered with all his voice, and Number Five of Harvard turned a drawn face to this salutation so close at hand, and in a quick glance recognized his dethroned rival, whom he had once met on the lawn at Gales Ferry. The man in the boat flashed a smile of comradeship to the man in the launch, and both felt better for the incident.

Cynthia was clapping her hands, then she tore the violets from her gown and flung them as far as she could toward the distant crew.

"Yale! Yale!" she cried. "Cast off. I want to work the launch down that way to see them. Wasn't it glorious? Oh, I never saw anything half so fine. I want to shake their hands, every one of that beautiful, blessed crew. I'd give ten years of my life to be one of those men at this moment."

She had not looked at Jack, but he was determined to obtrude himself somehow.

"How about the man who worked just as hard, and gets none of this hero worship? Doesn't he deserve anything from you?"

"Poor old Jack!" she said tenderly. "Why, I forgot all about you for a little while. It is a shame you are not there. You ought to have tried just a little bit harder, hadn't you? Now you can't be a hero, but don't you care. We are all sorry as sorry as can be."

The launch had daringly poked a passage close to the float on to which the crew was now clambering from the shell. Big brown, half-naked men were hugging each other, and clumsily dancing in stockinged feet. Eagerly Cynthia asked her companion:

"Do tell me which is which, Jack. I want to be able to know them all by name. Which is the Stroke, and which is the man at Number Five? I want to see if he looks like you."

Hastings gave the information very soberly. The Stroke caught sight of his clouded face, and yelled to his fellows:

"Hey, here's Jack Hastings! Three long cheers for him. Are you ready?"

The cheer given by men still struggling to regain their normal breathing came so gratefully to John Hastings that he felt like whimpering, because *they* understood. The launch was deftly steered alongside the float, and grabbing the outstretched hand of Hastings, the Stroke nearly pulled him overboard, as he whispered:

"Jack, I am glad you could see the race with the Only One. It must have helped you over the rough places. There is nothing like it when things look blue. God bless you both. Where is your mother? Be sure to come down to New Haven to-night, won't you?"

The Stroke jumped to help load the oars on the coaching launch just as Cynthia said to Hastings:

"Why didn't you present me? I think you are a stupid old Jack."

Where was his mother? Guilty and ashamed, he stammered:

"Please set me ashore anywhere as soon as you can, and I shall be eternally grateful."

She pouted.

"Do you want to leave me so soon? Certainly, I will put you ashore if you wish. You have been as cross as a bear. You must do penance by coming off to dinner to-night."

"Thanks, I have another engagement," said he shortly.

The observation train had gone to the station, and it must be emptied of its freight by this time. There was no more time for talk with Cynthia, and he did not know what else to say to her to whom the day was an outing, vastly exciting and enjoyable. Still, he sought one last word of sincere realization of his ill fortune, and found no response to his own heart hunger. He said "Good-bye," as he stepped ashore, and holding her hand for a moment:

"I am glad that you have had such a pleasant afternoon, Cynthia. A friend in need is a friend indeed."

The tribute touched and pleased her, and the irony of it wholly escaped her, as she gayly called after him:

"Be sure you don't forget to look us up to-night."

## VI

Hastings did not look behind him, as with lowered head he ran along the railroad track to the station, jumped into a cab and urged the driver to speed to the house where his mother must be waiting.

Some one within heard his footstep, knew it for what she craved most to hear, and was in the doorway of her room, when he saw her. Picking her up like a child, he covered her white hair, her tired face, her hands with kisses, and as she clung weeping on his breast, he carried her to a big armchair in the bay window. He was on his knees with his rumpled head in her lap when she found broken voice to say:

"Oh, Jack, are you well? Are you all right? My own precious boy! I have come to comfort and love you. Nothing else matters. Nothing else matters to me, now that I have found you safe and sound."

She twisted her slim fingers in his thick brown hair, and as she felt the warm pressure of his head in her lap, the years had stepped aside, and he was the little boy who used to flee to that dear sanctuary in every time of trial. And to her this was only another trouble, which only Mother could understand and clear from his path. When at length he looked up, she was shocked to see the shadow circles under his eyes, and the nervous twitching of the mouth that was so very like his mother's. He was sobbing, and not ashamed of it, as he murmured:

"I have been disgraced and disappointed, but I don't care any more now that I have found you. Are you all right, Little Mother? Did you think I had deserted you?"

She told him of the race as she had seen it, and was with difficulty dissuaded from planning to search out the Head Coach, crying with the angry sparkle he loved of old:

"It is not ladylike, Jack, but I would like to scratch his horrid eyes out. Of course, he should have kept you on the crew, but we are not going to cry over spilt milk, are we? I want you to tell me all about it—everything—so that we can look and find some consolation. Every cloud has a silver lining."

While he carried the tale down to the parting with Cynthia she smiled and frowned in turn, and wiped her eyes before he had finished. A mother's intuition read between the lines and when the rueful confession halted, her arm stole around his neck, and she kissed him again.

"It is a sad story," she said; "but never let me hear that word disgrace as long as you live. Of course, I was nearly killed about it to-day, and I should have been crying for four nights at sea if I could have heard the news before I started. But it would have been only because you were unhappy and disappointed. What else are mothers for than to understand when the world seems upside down? When you were seven years old, you were kept home from a Sunday-school picnic by the chicken-pox, and you told me in floods of tears that you didn't 'b'lieve you could never, never be happy again.' I knew how small your world was, and that the chicken-pox was big enough to fill it to overflowing.

"Now you have tried your best, you rowed as well as you knew how, and the crew was everything to you, just as it ought to be. But some day you may have larger troubles, and they, too, shall pass away, and more and more you will come back to the simple gospel of living I have tried to teach you, that there is only one standard by which to judge success or failure. Is the thing worth while, and have you done your best in the best way to gain it? I don't mean to preach, my boy mine. You don't want that. You want your mother. I know, I know."

She stroked his cheek as he went deep into his heart, and brought up more than he had ever told her before of his dreams of love, first love, and of what he had been building. His mother knew that she must be careful, and she hesitated, as if pondering how best to speak her view-point.

"She did not understand, poor girl. It is not all her fault, and it is not yours, laddie boy. When the race began and I saw that you were not in the crew, it seemed as if I were in the depths of a bad dream. I was with you all the way, and I thought of nothing else. And I know that while you would have been with me if you could, yet if the girl were here you would wish in your heart to find her first. No, don't try to deny it. But she did not know at all what it meant to you, she could not know. But if she had loved you, she would have understood as I did. We will talk about her all night if it will make your heartache any better. What are we going to do now?"

The boy straightened himself and threw back his wide shoulders, because his mother saw no cause for reproach in his downfall. But he did not want to see the crew again, and he wished to avoid the riotous celebration soon to burst. Obviously the best plan was to go to New Haven at once, where they could find refuge in his rooms, and pack his trunk for the vacation departure.

To him this little journey from New London was a panic flight, to her it was made radiant by the one fact that her boy had come back to her. After dinner, in a quiet corner of the college town, they went to his rooms on the campus. The sight of the two twelve-foot oars on the walls, his own trophies of two victories, their handles stained dark with the sweat of his hands, made her turn to him as they entered:

"Nothing can ever take those away from you, with all their splendid story of success."

The boy looked at them for an instant, then brushed a hand across his tired young eyes.

"Better make kindling of them," he said. "Look at that one over there. I won it as a raw, overgrown Freshman, and three years later I can't do as well as I did then. Matthews, 'the sub,' will hang my third oar on his wall next year. I am going to curl up on the window-seat and rest a while, Mother. I feel all played out."

She, too, was very tired, but felt that her son had need of her, and she tried to soothe him to sleep, and smiled as she found herself half unconsciously humming a slumber-song she had crooned to him twenty years before. Her photograph was on his desk, and framed near it the winsome face of Cynthia Wells, and she crossed the room to look closely and comprehendingly at the girl who had acted in her own world as naturally as had the youth in his. When she returned to the window, her son was asleep, and she softly kissed him.

Looking across the green, she saw a blaze of red fire that colored the evening sky. Rockets and Roman candles began to spangle the illumination, and presently the far-away blare of a brass band crept nearer. She knew that these were signs of the home-coming of the crew, of the celebration whose glories Jack had eloquently portrayed. It was not disloyalty to him that she should want to see what it was like, although she knew he would not want to be there. Yet feeling traitorish qualms, she scribbled a little note, saying she had gone out for a "breath of fresh air," and stole down the staircase.

When she came to the corner the procession was rioting up Chapel Street toward the campus. The band preceded a tally-ho, on top of which were the heroes in their white boating uniforms, nervously dodging innumerable fiery darts aimed straight at them by wild-eyed admirers on the pavement. Behind, surging from curb to curb, skipped thousands of students and townspeople, arm in arm, in common rapture. The wavering line of fireworks told that the tail of the parade was blocks and blocks away.

The coach was stopped at the corner of the campus, as a hundred agile figures swarmed up the wheels, and dragged the crew to earth, from which they were instantly caught up, and borne on tossing shoulders to the stone steps of the nearest recitation hall. There they were held aloft, still struggling, while cheers greeted each by name.

## VII

Now the celebration programme would have been halting and inadequate if the Assistant Manager of the Yale Navy had not hurried to New Haven on an earlier train. He had been in the car with John Hastings, and took it for granted that the sweet-faced woman of the silvery hair must be his mother. He was plunging through the crowd on the stone steps, trying to rescue the oarsmen in order to head them toward the banquet hall, when beneath the are light on the corner, a little way out of the tumult, he saw the timid lady for whom he had felt much sympathy. The Assistant Manager was ably fitted for his official task of looking after details, because he fairly boiled over with initiative, and with him to think was to act, as the powder speeds the bullet. He dashed across to Mrs. Hastings, and said, with a hurried and apologetic bow:

"Beg pardon, but this is Jack Hastings' mother, are you not? Yes, thank you, I was sure of it. It may seem presumptuous, but I have heard lots about you, and Jack has convinced me that you are the finest mother in the world, bar one. I have been so infern—so very busy since I got in town from New London, that I have had no time to look up Jack. We want him at the dinner, everybody does, and we want you just as much. In fact, you must be my special guest, and hear the speeches, anyhow, if you won't stay any longer. Jack's asleep, is he? Well, we'll wake him up, all right."

The alarmed little mother tried to protest several things at once. Jack had sworn he would not go to the dinner, and that he would break the neck of the man who should try to rout him out. Of course, Jack would not do that really, but he was all worn out and needed the rest. Please not to disturb him, and she would not dream of going without him, and she did not want to go at all. Her earnestness was almost tearful, but the Assistant Manager, who had heard perhaps the first ten words, darted off and was back with two young men whose fists were full of cannon crackers. He had each fast by the coat-collar, and shoving them into the foreground like a pair of marionettes, he breathlessly blurted:

"Mrs. Hastings, may I present Mr. Stower and Mr. 'Stuffy' Barlow, both Seniors, highly dignified and proper persons? This is Jack Hastings' mother. You are to escort Mrs. Hastings down to Harmonium Hall, and see that she has a nice seat in the gallery or near the door. No trouble at all, Mrs. Hastings, I assure you. Awfully glad to have had the honor of meeting you. Good-bye. I'll run over to Jack's room and drag him down there in five minutes."

Mrs. Hastings had all the sensations of being kidnapped. She tried to protest, even to resist, but was like a leaf caught up in a torrent, as Messrs. Barlow and Stower, both talking at once, handed her politely but firmly into the depths of a hack, climbed in after her and slammed the door.

Almost in a twinkling, as it seemed to the agitated mother, she was being ushered carefully into a small music gallery overlooking the banquet floor, where from a shadowy corner she could overlook the festivities in semi-seclusion. She waited only until her genial abductors were out of sight, and then slipped furtively toward the stairs, intending, of course, to return to her boy if he did not appear forthwith. Uneasy and fluttering, she was also keenly interested, for had not John placed this picture before her, and what it had meant to him in other years? He met her at the top of the stairway, looking sheepish and alarmed. She tried to explain, but he cut her short with a laugh:

"I know all about it, Little Mother. You fell a victim to the wiles of a terrible set of villains. You couldn't help yourself. Neither could I, when I heard how you had been spirited away. Now you are going to stay and see the fun, aren't you?"

She tried to persuade him to leave her and take his seat with the celebrants.

"No, I have lost my seat," said he, with the old shadow on his face. "I don't belong there any more.... I don't want to be seen. But the fellows promised not to give me away. It is pretty nervy for me to come at all. But I am here only to escort you."

She took his hand and held it while they sat well back in a corner of the gallery and watched the company trooping in. To the young oarsmen, so clean-cut and strong, tired but happy, all their woes and fears forgotten, this was their day of days. In a long row were seated the University eight, the substitutes, and the Freshman crew, which had also won its race. At the head of the table was "Big Bill" Hall, stout oarsman of thirty years ago, now a much stouter citizen. The captain of the crew was at his right, and at his left hand the beaming Head Coach, burned as black as any Indian. In another group were the younger coaches, most of them old strokes and captains, and mighty men at Yale in their time. Other oarsmen of other days were welcomed, regardless of the formality of invitation. Perhaps forty men around the board had known the test of the four-mile course, brothers of the oar through nearly two generations of rowing history.

The outcast was able to keep his poise until the Glee Club quartette rose to sing, by special request of the Head Coach, "Jolly Boating Weather." The first tenor had a sweet and sympathetic voice, and he had heard the story of the singing of this song on the float just before the race, wherefore he did the verses uncommonly well.

Then the old fellows, some with grizzled thatches, and some with thatches scant and thin, had their innings and pounded the table to emphasize their harmonious declaration that

"Twenty years hence such weather

Will tempt us from office stools.

We may be slow on the feather,

And seem to the boys old fools,

But we'll still swing together———"


The song carried to Hastings was the last straw to break the endurance which had pulled him through the long, long day. He did not want his mother to see his quivering lip, and he thought she would not perceive that he was near to breaking down. Did she know? Why, she felt his emotion in the hand she clasped tighter than before, she read his thoughts in the very beat of his pulse, and when he whispered that he must have caught a cold in the head because he was getting an attack of sniffles, she needed no words to enlighten her understanding. If his tears were those of a boy, then she thanked God she was childish enough to feel with him at every step and turn of the way that was blocked by the biggest sorrow of his life. She asked him whether he would like to go home. He shook his head and said that he would stick it through to the end.

## VIII

Speeches were in order, and the presiding alumnus hove himself out of his chair, and hammered the table with the rudder of the winning shell, thoughtfully lifted and provided by the able Assistant Manager. There were cheers for "Big Bill" Hall, of the '73 crew, more cheers for Yale, and before the uproar was quiet his great voice rose above it as he began to speak. Presiding Judge of the Supreme Court of a New England State when at home, he was all a Yale man come back to his own upon such occasions as this, and because Yale men loved him they called him "Big Bill."

"When we get into the big world beyond the campus," he began, "it may seem to some that this intensity of purpose, this absorption in a sport, were childish, yet we do not regret those convictions, we are proud of them, for these same qualities make for manhood in the larger duties of a wider horizon. And, after all, are the things for which we are striving in after years any more worth while? Are they always sweetened and uplifted by so much devotion, unselfishness, loyalty, and singleness of purpose? Are they thrilled by as fine a spirit of manliness? We hear it said that the old Yale spirit is losing its savor, that men are working for themselves rather than for the college, that they hold in light esteem things that were sacred and vital to us. I do not believe these criticisms are true.

"The young man I wished most to see is not here to-night. He would not come to help us celebrate a victory over an ancient and honorable foe. He believes that he has lost the respect of his comrades and that he has been proven a failure. For three years he has been a University oar. This season he could not keep his weight down to the limit of former years, he found that he could not keep up with the eight—although he tried as never before—and he was not helping the crew. The day came when he had to be removed, and he experienced as bitter disappointment as could befall a young man of spirit and pluck. The coaches and captain expected that he would throw up training, leave the Quarters and go home. It was the natural thing to do, because he was cut to the soul, and it was like attending his own funeral services to hang around the place.

"Without a word he slipped into the place of a substitute, and did a substitute's work as long as there was need of it. I venture to say that he would have scrubbed out the boathouse if it would have been of service to the crew. Do you know why he took this stand? Not because he did not care, but because he cared so much. When he offered to help as a substitute he said:

"'If I can help the Yale shell to go faster by being out of it, I am glad of it. That is what I am rowing for. And if I can be of any use as a substitute, why, that is what I am here for, too. It is all for Yale, isn't it?'

"He did not know that he was overheard. It was not meant to be overheard. But it expressed his whole attitude, and he stood by it to the end. You youngsters who licked Harvard to-day deserve all the praise and rejoicing that comes to you. We are all proud of you, and we know how hard and well you have worked. But while you are the heroes of this celebration, *the* hero did not row with you. His name is 'Jack' Hastings, the man who was glad to help a Yale crew go faster by getting out of it.

"And when you hear it said that the Yale spirit is dying out, I want you to think of that remark. That man absorbed the spirit right here that made him take that view as a matter of course. It was because he did not think of anything else to be done under the circumstances that he epitomized the spirit that will make this old place great as long as it stands. Endowments and imposing buildings can never breed that spirit. It grows and blossoms as the fruitage of many generations of tradition, and when Yale loses it, she is become an empty shell, a diploma factory, and no longer a nursery of the right kind of manhood needed in this country.

"Three long cheers for 'Jack' Hastings, who, if he did not help to win this race, will help to win races long after he is gone from the campus world; and so long as his words are remembered Yale men on football field, on track and diamond, and on the dear old Thames will feel their inspiration. Are you ready?"

The men rose the length of the table and shouted, with napkins waved on high. Before the last "rah, rah, rah, Hastings, Hastings, Hastings," subsided, the Assistant Manager had become red in the face and exceedingly uneasy. He wrestled with a weighty ethical problem, because while he had pledged his word not to reveal the secret of Hastings' presence within sight and sound of this ovation, he realized that to lead him in would be a crowning and dramatic episode. A compromise was possible, however, and he slipped around the table and whispered in the ear of "Big Bill" Hall.

In the gallery the little mother had shrunk farther back into the shadows, half afraid of this uproar, yet happier than ever before in her life. She looked at her boy, sitting close beside her, his face hidden so that she could not see the illuminating joy in it, the dazed look of unreality, as if he were coming through dreamland. There was no surprise in her mind. Of course, this triumph was no more than what was due, and she could have hugged the massive chairman as a person of excellent discernment. The boy whispered:

"He does not really mean it, Mother. There is some mistake. He has been out of college so long that he does not know what things mean."

She patted his burning cheek and whispered:

"Why, I knew it all the time. But you would not believe it if your mother said you were a hero. I wonder how the Head Coach feels now? I wish I——"

With a quick leap Jack had wrenched himself away and was clattering down the stairs. He had seen the whispered conference and "Big Bill" Hall staring up at the gallery, and fearing that he was trapped and betrayed, he fled into the street and was running for the nearest corner before the Assistant Manager could pass through the hall to the foot of the stairs. The conspirator had not promised silence regarding Hastings' mother, and before she knew what was happening he was by her side, so quickly that she thought it was Jack returned to her. As she looked up in alarm, the Assistant Manager had her reluctant hand, and was insisting upon leading her to the railing of the little gallery. She gazed at the upturned faces, and there was a moment of expectant silence. Then Judge Hall shouted the command: "Three long cheers for Jack Hastings' mother."

She was trembling now, and the lights and faces below swam in a mist of tears, as she timidly bowed. Then, as the full realization of the tribute swept over her like an engulfing wave, she became youthfully erect, she smiled, and blew kisses with both her slender hands toward the long table. She was thanking them in behalf of her boy, that was all, because they too understood. Certain that he must be waiting not far away, she bowed again, and hurried down the stairs, meeting the Head Coach in the hall. His face was serious, his manner abashed, as he said:

"I want to ask whether you will shake hands with me, Mrs. Hastings. I am proud that you do me the honor. I wish to tell you something more than you have heard to-night, and I am going to tell it to all the men, when I return to the room. Your son was too heavy to handle himself as well as he did last year and the year before. But I believe he would have rowed in the race if a mistake had not been made. I found out when it was too late that his rigging, or measurements, in the shell was not right for him, and it would have made considerable difference if he could have been shifted in time. It was wholly my fault, and nobody else was to blame in any way. I can never make it up to him, and my only consolation is that you have found what I have learned, that he is a good deal finer man than we thought him, and an honor to Yale beyond all the rest of us. You must hate me, more than any one else in the world. I remember how my mother shared my joys and sorrows in the crew."

The mother put out her hand again, and clasped that of the Coach, as she said simply, but with a catch of emotion in her voice:

"I did hate you to-day. I thought you had broken my boy's heart. Now I have to thank you. God's ways are not our ways, and I rejoice that while I have lost a captain of the crew, I have gained a man, every inch of him, tried in the fire and proven. This is the happiest night of my life. I would rather have heard the speech of Judge Hall, and the cheers that followed it, than to have my son in four winning crews and captain of every one of them. Of course he is a hero. Didn't you know that?"

The Head Coach started to speak, when the elbow of "Big Bill" Hall nudged him. The bulk of him filled the passage-way, and his voice boomed out into the night:

"If you don't bring that boy around to the hotel to see me in the morning, I will take back all I have said about him, Mrs. Hastings. Now I know where he gets all his fine qualities."

She blushed and courtesied, and the two men escorted her to the pavement, as John Hastings slipped from a doorway across the street and came over to them. His mother's escort, believing that he had been no nearer the banquet than this, made a rush for him, which he nimbly dodged, and slipped his mother's arm in his.

"He is mine now," said she. "He has a previous engagement, and, besides, I don't want him spoiled. Good-night to you. Come along, Jack, you are not too big to mind your mother, are you?"

The two walked slowly across the Green toward the campus. The communion of their uplifted souls was perfect, their happiness almost beyond words. She was first to break this rare, sweet silence, and strangely enough, she said nothing about the vindication and the triumph. Looking up into his face she almost whispered:

"Are you caring so much that Cynthia disappointed you to-day, dear boy of mine? Does it hurt and rankle? I could see it in your eyes to-night. Do you want to marry her very much? Are you sure of your heart?"

He winced a little and held her arm tighter than before, as he replied:

"Little Mother, it has been my first real love story, as you know. The thought of her has helped me over many a rough place. Before to-day she was always so quick to understand. And—and she seemed to like me better than any other fellow she knew. I was fairly aching to be worthy of her, to make my place in the world for her. I wasn't conceited enough to think she loved me. I was only hoping that some day—Any man has a right to do that, has he not?"

It was not easy for the mother to say what she wished to tell him, but at length her response was:

"I don't want you to think I am criticising her, or sitting in judgment, but you must not let her mar your faith and hope and happiness. I want to help you to guard those precious gifts. You must not blame her too much. You have been believing that she understood you, because you would have it that way. She is no older than you, a girl of twenty, accustomed to a wholly different life from yours. She was flattered by your attention, for you were a great man in her eyes. She liked you because no one can help liking you. But it made a difference when you were a hero knocked off his pedestal. And yet you expected to find in her sympathy a balm that even your mother could not give. Poor lad, mothers are handy sometimes, but most boys do not find it out until their mothers are gone from them."

"I thought I knew her so well," said he, after another silence. "It looks as if I had amused her and nothing more. But I have found you, and I have fallen head over heels in love with you, Little Mother, all over again, and I am going to kiss you right under this electric light."

Even yet she was not sure that she had sounded the depths of the ache in his heart, but as she looked up at the light in his campus rooms she said softly:

"Some day you will understand, and will thank God your mother understood. He giveth you the victory unforeseen."

# CORPORAL SWEENEY, DESERTER

"I'll be gettin' five years—five years at least."

The surging fear became fixed in these words, and they, in turn, swung in with the cadenced tramp of Corporal Sweeney, the other prisoner, the sentry, and the young lieutenant along the Chien-men Road toward the American camp and the guard-house. As the refrain rolled itself over in the brain of the corporal, he discovered that he was muttering it aloud when the other prisoner said explosively:

"I know you will, and so will I; but, by ----, I'm going to make a run for it!"

"You're the silliest fool in Peking if you do," replied the corporal. "An' where would you be after runnin' to? No place to——"

He checked himself and turned his head. The sentry and the lieutenant were at their heels, but in the clamor of the crowded thoroughfare the talk had been unheard. A swirl of Chinese street merchants was scattering from in front of a German wagon-train, a troop of Bengal Lancers clattered recklessly into the ruck, and the road flung the tangled traffic to and fro between its walls, like a tide in a mill-race. The corporal muttered again to the scowling man beside him:

"Nothin' doin'. Sure to be captured this side Tientsin. Forget it. You're crazier than thim——"

A shout in his ear made him jump aside, and he saw the sentry lurch against the flank of a transport camel and lose his footing as a cart-wheel struck him from behind. The loaded rifle fell on the chaotic stone flagging. The other prisoner heard the crash and knew what it meant. Here seemed the chance he sought, but instead of doubling into one of the crooked side streets, he broke away down the middle of the Chien-men Road, and the traffic opened up for him, as the crowd, grasping as by instinct what was happening, scattered in panic.

The young lieutenant whipped his revolver from its holster and took a snap-shot at thirty yards, not caring overmuch if a Chinese got in range of the heavy bullet. As he fired, the fugitive seemed to trip and catch himself, then ran a few steps farther, falling all the time, until he crumpled up in the filthy mud of the pavement. The lieutenant stood looking at his quarry, his eye still ranging along the barrel of the revolver, while the sentry had picked up his muddy rifle, and, feeling faint and shaky, watched a private of his own regiment become, in an instant, something that looked like a roll of blankets doubled under the feet of the Chinese street mob.

The two had forgotten the corporal, who stood beside them as intent as they upon the pitiable tragedy; and the three appeared to be posing for a military tableau. But almost as swiftly as death had come to the escaping prisoner, there swept over the one that remained a frenzy of desire to run. He knew how remote was the possibility of freedom, how desperately small the chance against recapture, dead or alive. But hammers were beating in his head the cadence of "I'll be gettin' five years—five years at least." And the opportunity was made by another's unwilling sacrifice.

*The flight of Corporal Sweeney.*

The corporal was unconscious of a voluntary act, and something seemed swiftly to drag him, as he wheeled and dashed for the entrance of an alley not more than ten yards away. A peddler's shoulder-yoke was splintered against his shoulder, and he thought that the bruising impact was the shock of the expected bullet; the yells of the sweetmeat-sellers at the alley's mouth sounded like the outcry he dreaded to hear; but the lieutenant and the sentry turned in time to see only the trail of sprawling Chinese left in the wake of the escaping prisoner. The sentry jumped in pursuit, stumbled into the tortuous alley, and saw a blank wall ahead. Between that and the Chienmen Road three lanes twisted off to left and right, and he ran up the nearest one at random.

Somewhere beyond the huddled houses, he could hear the thud of leather-shod feet, the staccato flight of which marked the trail of the deserter; but the pursuer could find no way through or around. When he entered the street beyond, there was no blue overcoat in the crowded field of vision, and the shuffling sound of felt-soled native shoes gave no clew. He returned to the lieutenant, genuinely weary and speciously disappointed. The officer was leaning over the body of the other prisoner, and there was keen unhappiness in his flushed young face.

"I've found an empty cart," he said to the sentry. "Help me carry this poor fellow to camp. He has no use for a doctor. As for Sweeney, he can't get away. He's hiding in the American section, and I will get the provost-marshal over the field 'phone from headquarters, and have the guard sweep the district from end to end. The man will be captured before morning."

This occurred to the fugitive, also, as certain to happen, when he staggered through a little courtyard, far in the heart of the "Chinese City," and fell into a corner of a smoke-fogged room. It was so nearly nightfall that the one occupant, failing to recognize the headlong visitor, yelled and scuttled away from the brazier which he was trying to coax into warmth against the winter night.

"It's me—all same me—come back. You no sabee this American soldier if men come to look see me," gasped the corporal.

The Chinaman nodded without speaking and slipped out. Sweeney was fighting for breath, and the fumes of coal-gas in the fetid room were suffocating him. He tore a hole in the side wall of oiled paper, and gulped his lungs full of the frosty night air. It was the room from which he had gone the day before, when, after drinking much Japanese beer, he had bought a quart of *samshu* to carry away with him.

It was the deadly, maddening samshu that had caused the downfall of Corporal Sweeney, and now he was trying to remember what had happened in the twenty-four hours before he had been marched down the Chien-men Road with the other prisoner. He knew that he had overstayed his leave, but that was a minor matter compared with the row in the canteen on Legation Street. He recalled that an American officer had entered the place to investigate the uproar, and the corporal's mind held a blurred picture of himself conspicuously cursing his superior officer with black oaths, and struggling to "knock the face off him." Then he had fled, to be picked up later by the lieutenant who had shot and killed Private Smathers on the way to camp.

The corporal drew back from the hole in the paper wall, and slumped down on the floor, a Chinese blue blouse tucked under his aching head.

"An' five years more, for attempted escape," he groaned, "an' two clane enlistments behind me, an' promotion a cinch in the next six months. Never a coort martial ag'in' me. It was all the —— samshu. Serves a white man right for foolin' with haythen liquor. An' they'll be pullin' me out of here in no time at all. Holy Mother! where kin I go?"

The disgraced soldier turned as a new dread smote him.

"An' the Boxer swine that kapes this poison-shop will be handin' me over as soon as he hears the news of the shindy down the Chien-men Road."

Panic fear caught hold of the corporal, body and soul, and he wrestled with it in the darkness. He knew not whither to turn. Hiding among the Chinese in the city was impossible, and to take to the open road meant capture at Tientsin or Taku if he made his way that far in a flight toward the seacoast. To go blindly into the country about Peking, unarmed and penniless as he was, knowing perhaps five words of Chinese, was to drag out the finish in slow starvation, or to be picked up by a foreign outpost, or to fall among hostile natives. He was as helpless as a castaway adrift on a raft in mid-ocean. The penalties of capture or surrender seemed worse than any sort of death, for Corporal Sweeney had been a good soldier, bred to a hardy outdoor life.

The disgrace tortured him, and either alternative of his situation was unthinkable. Yet after three hours of trembling in his trap, he would have welcomed the chance of flight into the open, beyond the walls of the nightmare city. The Chinese landlord had not returned, and it seemed likely that intruders had been warned away from the smoky room with the hole in the oiled paper of the side wall. The deserter had found a bottle of samshu, and tried to brace his nerves with a swallow of it, but the smell sickened him, and he flung it against the brick partition, in a passion of rage at the source of his cyclonic ruin. The heavy, yellow liquid guttered across the floor, and the stench of it drove the soldier into the courtyard, where the chatter of Chinese voices sent him quaking back into his little inferno.

He was not a coward, but he was alone in the darkness with such fears as wrested from him all weapons. Somewhere outside, a Chinese watchman, drifting along on his rounds, was beating a gong to frighten away evil-doers. The measured *bong, bong, bong* caused the fugitive to wish that sudden death might overtake the harmless old gentleman, for at each stroke it seemed as if tacks were being driven into his skull. Toward midnight Corporal Sweeney fell into a stupor of complete exhaustion that was no more than a caricature of sleep. A scratching on the paper door and a falsetto whisper awoke him, and he sprang to his feet, striking out in the gloom, to ram his fist through the fragile panel into something yielding which cried:

"O-w-w—a-i-i! Me, master; You Han. Somet'ing do-ing, all l-l-ight?"

The deserter extended a muscular arm, grasped a handful of wadded coat, and dragged the visitor in with one lightning sweep. Then, trying to choke his amazed voice into a whisper, he croaked:

"Oh, me cock-eyed darlin' lad! An' how did you dig me out? I niver felt like kissin' a Chink before. Now get me out o' this, or I'll break your back over me two knees. I'm down an' out this time. Are you goin' to give me up for the sake o' the rewarrd?"

The boy, whom the corporal had picked up, a starving outcast from a plundered village, on the march to Peking, tried to tell what he knew in painfully Pidgin English, shattered by his master's interruptions. He had learned that the corporal was a day overdue in camp, and had started out to find him early that morning. Then came the tragedy and the escape, the tidings of which were brought to the camp with the body of Private Smathers. You Han had heard the name "Sweeney" scattered through the excited talk of the company, until he pieced together a working impression of what had happened. He had ransacked canteens, tea-houses and gambling-dens from the camp to the Tatar city wall until he began to pick up the trail from groups at the street corners who had seen the "madman runaway soldier."

The corporal chopped the narrative short, because he was not interested in the way of his fall into the bottomless pit, but in an agony of speculation regarding the new possibility of a way out. The coming of You Han made him clutch the hope of the open country, anywhere, anyhow, no matter what lay beyond. The thought of flight alone among the millions of mysterious aliens had oppressed him horribly. You Han had the fidelity of a dog for the domineering American soldier, whose ways he did not understand, but, because they were his ways, they were believed to be impeccable. Now his lord had done something more extraordinary than usual, for which, it appeared, decapitation threatened. In addition to blind obedience, You Han knew what samshu was, and was ready to make large allowances. It was only this new tone of entreaty, almost of supplication, that alarmed the servant. Corporal Sweeney shook off the paralyzing grip of his fears long enough to give You Han orders in a voice that still quavered in little broken gasps:

"You get Peking cart, quick? Qui-qui—chop-chop—chase yourself—sabee? Have you got any money in thim flowin' robes?"

You Han flashed a bisecting grin that was like splitting a sheet of parchment, and dove into a knotted sash, where the clink of silver made reply. Then he was gone, and the deserter became instantly submerged in the returning rush of his manifold terrors. It seemed years before he heard the protesting shrieks of a cart axle and the rattle of harness in the compound. You Han stole in, and half dragging the corporal to the cart, helped him to crawl under the curtained hood, whispering:

"One piecee cart belong my cousin. No pay him. You stay bottom side. We go countlee."

As the cart jolted into the alley, the man beneath the cover heard, faint and far, the beat of cavalry hoofs on the frozen earth. They were coming nearer, and the fugitive flattened himself under a pile of quilts, while the sweat beaded on his face. In a few moments the clink of sabers and the creaking of saddle-leathers were audible, and the patrol wheeled into a side street so close to the jogging cart that the deserter caught the voice of a Sixth Cavalry trooper objecting:

"It's a blazin' cold night to be pokin' in all the rat-holes of Peking for as good a blank-blanked son of a gun as Jack Sweeney. Wonder how he got up against it so hard."

The reply was lost, for the deserter's heart was whanging against his ribs and sounding louder to him than the clatter of cavalry. You Han drove the mule at a gallop and said no word except once, when he turned and remarked:

"Samshu no good, master. Floget it. Dlink water, all l-l-ight."

At daylight the cart was beyond the outer wall of Peking, heading west, as aimless a derelict as ever tossed in uncharted seas. You Han did not veer toward his own home on the Pei-ho, for he knew that it lay in the track of the traffic to Tientsin, and that over the ruins of his village floated the flag of an American infantry outpost. The dawn came clear and cold, but sad in the gray aspect of tenantless villages, and the litter of ungarnered millet-fields stretching over the flat lands to the horizon. The driver told the deserter that the last foreign outpost had been passed, and that he might get out and walk with safety. Half frozen, bitterly bruised from tossing between floor and roof of the springless cart, hungry and weak, the deserter climbed from his ignominious hiding-place and trudged in silence along the rutted highway. Presently You Han turned off the road, threaded a course through the yards of a shattered temple, and drew up by a marble altar.

"Have chow now," said he, and the summons to breakfast aroused a shadow of animation in the deserter. He knew not where the meal was coming from, but he was past wondering, and the Chinese youth was in full command of the sorry expedition. You Han crawled into the cart and produced a charcoal stove, dried fish, potatoes, and a teapot.

"All belong my cousin. He keep store; pay bimeby," said the boy, with what might have passed for a wink.

The companions ate in silence. Shame had begun to march in the foreground of the deserter's thoughts, crowding fear a little to the rear. The soldier of a conquering race was as helpless as a child in the hands of one of the conquered whom he had not considered wholly human, whose swarms had fled like rats before the path of the columns in khaki. The fugitive cursed and hated himself, possessed by an unmanly humiliation impossible to imagine a few hours before. The little dun mule munched dry millet-stalks, and squealed when You Han fetched him water from the temple well.

"I ain't got as much sand left in me as that sawed-off apology fer a mule," groaned the corporal; "an' he's a good deal more of a man than meself."

You Han resumed the march without consulting his lord, which made the deserter writhe anew, but he could say nothing. The cart trailed along the foot of an ancient military wall for several miles, while the man sullenly chewed the cud of bitterness and the boy revolved great things in his unruffled mind. You Han was about to venture on some fragmentary consolation, when the deserter, who was walking a little in advance, balked in his tracks and stood crouched as if he had seen a rattlesnake. The dun mule snorted and fanned his ears like an agitated jack-rabbit. A furlong beyond, the steel ribbons of a railway track cut across the road and vanished in sandy cuttings. Corporal Sweeney looked instinctively for a telegraph line and saw one wire threading the skyline in a humming loop. The sight hurled him back to the Chien-men Road and the lieutenant alertly picking off Private Smathers with a long snap-shot.

"What's this fool railroad doin' here? I wonder are they consthructin' it to ketch up with me? Come a-runnin' there *pronto*,[A] chop-chop. Ain't there no gettin' away from annywhere?"

[A] Soldiers who have campaigned in the Philippines use the word *pronto* for "hurry up" or "hustle."

He volleyed the questions at You Han as if they had been jerked out of him. The boy looked puzzled as he replied:

"Devil cart go Pao-ting-fu, then go Peking. No belong to Amelican soldier. English have got."

They crossed the rails on the run, as if the metals burned their feet, and the deserter flogged the mule into a gallop, until their road twisted beyond sight of the track and its unexpected autograph of a civilization they were fleeing headlong. He would not have dared predict it, but in the afternoon Corporal Sweeney began to be a man again. They had passed beyond the area laid waste by the Christian allies, and the villages were populous and busy. You Han had glimpsed a shadow of the shame that smoldered in his master's mind, and he was for making little overtures, simple yet crafty, to win him back to himself. As the first step in reconstruction, he called "Look-see, master!" and pulled from beneath the body of the cart a "Krag" rifle, bayonet, and cartridge-belt. The deserter threw back his shoulders at sight of them, and in an outburst of gratitude smote his benefactor so that his head ached for several hours.

"Last night, when get cart, go back camp," twittered You Han; "find one piecee master's gun in tent. Plenty dark. Sently shoot, no can hit. Good, by golly!"

"Good! you twenty-four carat jewel of Asia! You're the goodest imitation of a white man that was ever bound in yeller leather by mistake. Now I feel as if I wanst looked like a man meself. Give me a rag an' a bit o' that stinkin' cookin'-grease, an' make room on the carrt till I do up me house-cleanin'."

You Han grinned and began to wail an interminable song about a girl called "Little Fat Spring Fragrance," who lived in the "Village of the Wise and Benevolent Magistrate." The ballad rose shriller as the singer saw the corporal swinging along ahead, his rifle nestling on his squared shoulder as if it had come home to its own, his back as flat as a board. You Han was even more jubilant when his master spun on his heel, and shouted with the rasp of the drill-ground in his voice:

"Shut up that racket! It's worse 'n the carrt axle."

The bracing wind swept keen out of the Siberian north, and sunshine flooded from a cloudless sky. The deserter forgot much of his weariness, and caught himself whistling "assembly," but broke off with a groan.

Toward sunset the surrounding wall of a village was outlined like a rocky island in the level plain. You Han halted a ragged wayfarer, and coaxingly addressing him as "great elder brother," dragged forth the information that the town was of considerable size, and that in it was the residence of the ruler of the district. The song of the "Village of the Wise and Benevolent Magistrate" had suggested an inspiration whose magnitude made You Han gasp. But he took possession of it without flinching, and when they were within a mile of the gateway in the wall he said to the deserter:

"You wait. I go look-see."

The mule browsed by the roadside, the corporal sprawled near by, and the brave figure in blue cotton trudged on alone to the town, the strangeness of which made his heart flutter. He swaggered in past the outer wall, searched out the *yamen* of the district magistrate, and that dignitary graciously consented to see the importunate pilgrim. You Han kotowed before the heart-quaking presence in the gilded audience-room, and with wailing stammer delivered the oration composed on the cart:

"An illustrious and most honorable general of the foreign soldiers comes to visit your beautiful city. I am his insignificant and thrice-despised servant. This valiant and inexpressibly distinguished hero is of the Americans, who protect and do not plunder and destroy. He comes to extend peace and protecting power to your Heavenly Presence, and to learn whether you have been molested by other foreign-devil armies, whom he will swiftly punish if it be your august pleasure to ask it. My insufferably benevolent master leaves soldiers, cannon, horses behind him, lest he terrify the country round about, already in fear of the devastating foreign fighting-men. He sends the greetings of one ruler to another, and also his card."

You Han bobbed his head to the floor by way of incessant punctuation, and watching eagerly from the tail of his eye for results hopeful or otherwise, laid before the magistrate the vivid label of a tin of "Army Cut Plug," on which heroes in blue and khaki posed nonchalantly in a "baptism of fire." A group of official servants, crowding within ear-shot, saw a gleam of surprised pleasure twinkle through the huge spectacles of their ruler. They took their cue, and helping the trembling You Han to his feet, were soon bustling through the courtyard, propelled by vehement commands to make haste.

Half an hour later, the deserter saw approaching a procession led by You Han and a squad of yamen runners, whom he knew by the red tassels on their flat hats. These rode shaggy rats of ponies, and behind them tailed off scores of villagers on foot and convoys of squealing children. The American grabbed his rifle and dodged behind the cart, ready to run or open fire, until he heard You Han's shrill shouts of reassurance. Then he was swept up in an admiring throng, whose bodies doubled in homage, down to the wee tots who fell on their flat noses when they tried to kotow.

You Han had no time for explanations. He was expanding in the reflected glory of his own devising, and busy chasing children from under the agile hoofs of the ponies. In their layers of wadded coats, like so many puff balls, the jolly youngsters rolled to the roadside, and the deserter felt a stir of emotion which he could not have defined. Yes, there were homes and firesides and mothers and play and work and love in this land of desolation, and the smoke of the village hearths beckoned with vague homeliness.

The shopkeepers left their wares and the old men in the doorways tucked away their pipes when the procession filled the little streets, and the deserter rode to the yamen like a conquering hero. In the courtyard of the compound other servants waited to escort the "benevolent foreign general" to rooms made ready for him. There was fire in the brick *kang*, or sleeping-platform, and chickens, eggs, fruit and potatoes, and a fur-lined robe were heaped on a table. You Han vanished, and the outlaw sat himself down in speechless wonderment. Presently You Han returned and announced that the magistrate would be inexpressibly honored to receive the Personage in the evening, and the reason for not inviting him to dine was that he knew the guest would prefer his food prepared after his own strange fashion by his own servant. As in a gorgeous dream the deserter dined, with three attendants squabbling with You Han for the honor of passing each dish. Then he brushed his dusty leggings and blue clothes and summoned a barber.

A little later the guest was greeted as a person of rare distinction by the dignified elderly gentleman in red-silk robes who ruled and "squeezed" the district. The corporal rose grandly to the occasion. The two mingled to a nicety their mutual attitudes of respect, cordiality, protection. They talked laboriously through the doubtful medium of the overpowered You Han, whom the intricacies of the mandarin dialect bowled over from the one side, and on the other such instructions as these from the corporal:

"Tell old Four-Eyes that I'm the personal ripresintative of George Washington and Gineral Grant, an' that when I stamp me fut a million brave soldiers trimble violently; but that because I know a great intelleck when I see one, me heart is swelled with pride to sit down and talk it over as man to man. Poke that into him good and har-r-d."

The official volleyed many questions, and the deserter parried what fragments of them You Han was able to pass along. A military escort to the next village was offered, but the guest declined with polite emphasis. He was not seeking ostentation in public. When he went to his apartments after a surfeit of cakes, wine, and tobacco, Corporal John Sweeney rubbed his close-cropped head and puzzled over his identity. As he curled up on the warm brick kang, he was a deserter fast becoming reconciled to his fate.

"It strains the rivets of me imagination to believe it's rale. I hope there's more miracles in stock where this one was projuced," he murmured sleepily.

Just at dawn he awoke. There was a clatter of voices in the courtyard, and the sound of horses moving hurriedly. Presently the paper of the latticed wall was ripped, and a brown finger popped through. All the fears of the refugee came trooping back with squadrons reinforced. He ripped the door open, rifle in hand. A string of traders' ponies was filing out for an early start toward Peking, and a hostler stood with his face pressed against the hole in the wall, trying to catch a glimpse of the lordly foreigner. That was all. But the deserter saw again the smoky room in the "Chinese City," and heard the Sixth Cavalry squad wheel just in rear of his frantic flight. The "illustrious guest" was again the fugitive, escaping, he knew not whither, from "five years—five years at least."

He kicked the sleeping You Han into action, and the cart was under way as soon as the mule had fed.

"Only thirty miles from Peking," growled the corporal; "not half far enough. An' cavalry is prancin' out to loot, pacify, an' scatter Christian blessings with th' mailed fisht where they have no business to be thinkin' of. I hike till I drop, an' that's me ultimatum."

They pressed on all day until the dun mule swayed in the shafts and the pilgrims were ready to drop by the roadside. The night was passed in a village tavern, for You Han was too weary to organize a reception. The deserter slept fitfully, and awoke often talking to himself. Nervous and foot-sore, he took the trail at dawn of the third day, You Han watchful and worried. As the deserter turned frequently to look behind him, the aspect of the future crushed him, while the imminent past lashed him to persistent flight. Camp, and the close comradeship of men in blue and khaki; the routine round of his army years; the Chicago streets that had known his boyhood; the father and mother who were proud of his record—these and all other links in the chain of his thirty years were as if they had never been forged. Names, faces and scenes of which he had been an intimate part were in an obliterating distance, and nothing that had gone before was given strength to follow him, except the incidents of his escape, and these filled all the landscape with portents.

Soon they came to a schoolhouse in the middle of a tiny hamlet. You Han knew it for such when the refugees were rods away, since from the squat building came an incessant sound like the hum of a gigantic top. The children were reciting their daily task from the Confucian Analects at the limit of their lung power, when the foreigner was spied by a truant outpost, and the teacher could not hold the clamorous flock in leash. By scores they tumbled out to scamper off in terror until You Han shouted his message of good will and the corporal laughed, threw down his rifle, and became one of them. It was not long before uproarious applause greeted his attempts to play jackstones and strike the sharpened stick to make it fly into the miniature mud-pie "city."

Again the feeling of homeliness tugged at his heart, and he lingered among the children until the teacher gathered them in, with labor like that of collecting spilled quicksilver.

You Han swaggered into the next village beyond, with a port inspired by remembrance of the magistrate's yamen, but he came to grief at the hands of the village bully. There was no mistaking the character of this truculent ruffian. His garments were studiously awry, and his queue was loosely braided and coiled around his neck to show that he thirsted for combat. He resented the lofty bearing of the stranger, and the two clashed with disaster to the features of You Han, who was plucky but overmatched. He was rescued by the corporal, who gave the bully the worst beating of his career. The feat was applauded by a throng of villagers whose peace had been much disturbed by this chronic nuisance, and they feasted the hero at the house of the head man with complex and effusive hospitality. The wayfarers were pressed to stay and make the town their home for life.

This incident, coming in a sequence of revelations of the life of this hitherto despised people, set the thoughts of the deserter definitely into a new and hopeful channel.

"I begin to think," he said to You Han, "that I could stick it out in one of these back counties, at worst until the troops are l'avin' China in the spring. An' I could come pretty near to runnin' a town or two meself. One more day's march an' I'll risk stakin' out a claim for a while. An' I'll be a leadin' an' dignified citizen, an' grandfather by brevet to all the kids in the camp."

The advance was checked by the discovery that the cart axle had split and must be repaired to prevent a breakdown over the next bit of rough going. The corporal was in a bluster of impatience to press forward. Delay had not lost its power to frighten him. The next village lay ten miles beyond, but between was a desolate stretch of waste land in which no one lived, in which nothing grew. From the tiled roof of the tavern the corporal could see this little desert rolling like a lake almost from the village walls to the sky line. It caught his fancy with a huge onset of relief. Once beyond this barrier, he would feel secure against discovery, and he magnified it as the borderland of safety. You Han was surrounded by a group of voluble citizens who urged waiting two days until a new axle could be hewn from the solid tree; but the deserter exploded the conference by shouting:

"Dump the carrt here. Pack the mule, an' we'll send back for the Noah's ark when we get settled over beyant. Make haste an' upholster the mule with the baggage of light marchin' order."

When the dun mule, in tow of the boy, limped out of the gateway across the crumbling moat, its small hoofs sank to the fetlock in white sand, and the trail of cart-wheels winding across the plain shimmered in an aching dazzle of sunlight. At the end of an hour the village behind them was a brown smudge not more than two miles distant. The deserter made peevish comments, but there was cheerfulness in the crack of his profanity, as he plodded painfully ahead of the boy and the mule. Whenever they paused to rest he talked to You Han, not caring whether the boy understood one word in five. The two seemed alone in all the world; their calamitous fortunes were more closely knit than at any time in the flight; and hope lay somewhere beyond this barricade provided by a fate grown strangely kind.

"You'll have the next week to get the sand out o' thim foolish shoes o' yourn," observed the corporal. "An' me blisters will be attinded to by the chief surgeon of the county. Like chickens an' silk over-coats, my son? We're goin' hell-bent for the comforts of life by the carrt-load."

You Han talked to the mule in encouraging whistles and replied, "Can do," to the monologue of the corporal, who rambled on:

"Say, thim kids did me more good than a barrel o' monkeys. Weren't they corkers? By the holy poker! I'm goin' to marry you off to a little squeeze-toed fairy in the big town over the way, an' you'll live without worrkin' forevermore. Maybe the old man will follow suit. It's me life ambition to be idle an' palatial. An' You Han will be the hottest sport in fifty li. Dinghowdy? All right?"

In the third hour they were not more than halfway across, and the short winter afternoon was reddening. The level desolation had begun to tumble up into crowding little hills and sand barriers among which the trail now and then entangled itself. But the air was crystal and windless, and scrambling to the top of one of the white hills, the corporal could see the faintest tracery of a towered temple on the farther side of the desert as a guiding landmark. It was a forced march, and a halt was made only for a fragment of supper and a swig for man and mule from the water-bottle on the pack. The moon rose in the sleeping dusk, but before it was clear of the scalloping ridges of sand the sky became spattered with rags of flying cloud. Presently the wind behind the angry scud began to pick up gusts of sand and flirt them from one crest to another. The travelers rubbed their eyes and coughed as they plowed steadily westward, steering a course by the cart-trail, still discernible, and by the moon behind them. "We're more 'n halfway over," shouted the corporal, "an' it's silly to be dr'amin' of losin' ourselves in this two-by-four desert."

Then the gray sky closed down in blackness everywhere, and leaping billows of sand seemed to meet it. The rush of the terrific wind wiped out the trail as if it had been no more than a finger-mark. There were no more hills nor winding passages among them, only a fog of whirling sand. The wind had an icy edge as it brought the killing cold of Mongolian steppes a thousand miles away. The deserter and the boy covered their faces with their hands, their garments; and almost instantly they were adrift, cowering, lost, helpless. So dense was the driving smother of sand that they could scarcely see the mule straining at the end of its halter-rope. The hillocks were shifting with a complaining roar, and the shriek of the wind in mid-air was pierced with a shrill rasp like the commotion of innumerable iron filings.

The corporal and You Han groped toward the side of a hillock, seeking a lee; but the flooding sand tumbled down its side knee-deep, and the wind sucked round and searched them out, as if in chase. The flinty particles pelted in sheets, and bit their faces like incessant volleys of fine shot. There was no more time to think of what should be done than when a swimmer is plunged over a dam.

It did not seem possible that the danger of death was menacing in this absurdly small theater of action, yet it could not have been many moments before the deserter began to realize where lay the odds in another hour's exposure to such a storm. All sense of direction had been snatched from him, and he fought only for breath. You Han had no knowledge of desert storms in his home on the bank of the Pei-ho. He gasped whatever prayers came to him, but placed his active faith, still unshaken, in the ability of his master to save him from the choking, freezing terror. The man and the boy were not only stifled, but soon benumbed, for neither had ever felt anything to compare with the searching cold of this blast. They stumbled from one hill to another, sometimes keeping their feet, falling oftener, rising more slowly, the little mule trying in vain to turn tail to the storm.

There could be no conversation. At length the deserter muttered drowsily to the storm such fragments as these:

"No place like home. It's the finish that's comin' to me. Cudn't take me medicine like a man. P'rhaps this'll blow over soon. I'm blinded entirely. Good God! forgive me poor cowardly sowl! I niver meant to go wrong. Had to bring that poor fool You Han into this mess."

The deserter pitched forward on hands and knees, his rifle buried somewhere in his circling wake. He caught hold of You Han's queue lest they lose each other, and then the mule pushed impetuously between them, ears forward, muzzle outstretched, trumpeting joyfully.

"He b'lieve can find. He sabee plenty," feebly sputtered You Han.

The frantic mule dragged the boy by the lead-rope a few paces, the corporal falling, sliding after, and then stopped. The linked procession could go no farther. You Han collapsed in a little heap, and the corporal toppled face down. The boy had tied the lead-rope around his own wrist, and the impatient mule was jerking it so that the forlorn figure in the sand seemed to make appealing gestures. The corporal was without motion, and with a mighty effort You Han pulled himself a little nearer, and the mule followed protestingly. The swaying curtain of sand closed in around the three figures.

You Han struggled to his knees and with his teeth loosed the knotted cinch, and the pack fell from the mule. The boy writhed over on the corporal and tried to raise the dead weight, tried to talk to him in a wordless and appealing whimper. The deserter strove to rise, and failed until he dully comprehended that the boy sought to make him mount the mule, or at least to hitch him in tow with the lead-rope. Then the soldier awoke, and fighting off the death that had almost mastered him, lurched to one knee and pushed You Han toward the mule that was standing over them. His voice thick and rasping as if his tongue were of sandpaper, the deserter succeeded in saying:

"Get aboard that mule. No Chinese village in mine. Better man than me— you an' mule both better men. You won't? —— —— you, take that!"

The deserter swung his fist against the jaw of the struggling boy, and the blow went home with the last flicker of the old-time fighting strength of Corporal Sweeney. You Han dropped limp, as if shot. Then the fugitive from army justice braced himself, tried, and failed to lift the light body in his arms. Three times he tried and failed, and then, as the mule swerved, he fell against it and dropped the lad across its back, like a bundle of quilts. The cinch, trailing in the sand, tripped the man, and he slipped it over You Han and pulled it tight before he fell back in the tossing sand. The mule stumbled a step or two with its burden, found that it was free and in a moment tottered beyond the vision of the deserter.

Not more than a hundred yards away a camel-trail lay encamped against the storm, and to the Mongolian drivers, huddled in furs close to their beasts, came a little dun mule half dragging an unconscious Chinese youth, whom they took for dead as they wonderingly cut him loose from his lashing.

Daylight and the tail of the sand-storm had come before he was able to speak, and the camels were jostling into the line of march. The swarthy drivers scoffed at the story told by the raving stranger, until the bell-camel shied at something nearly buried in the sand. You Han fought the greedy northerners off until he had disclosed a figure in army blue and a clean-cut Irish face whose expression was vastly peaceful.

The last silver coin was gone from the knotted sash of You Han after he had persuaded the camel-men to carry the body to the village where Corporal Sweeney had expected to find a refuge from fear.

# THE LAST PILOT SCHOONER

Young James Arbuthnot Wilson slipped into the *Standard* building with an uneasy air as if he were vaguely on the defensive. Six months of work in the "City Department" had not rid him of the feeling of a cat in a strange garret. The veterans of the staff were rather pleased that this should be the attitude common among young reporters. It showed that the office machine was geared to high tension when every man, short of five years' service, was thankful to find his "job" had not slid from under him between two days.

Wilson could recall no specific warnings that his head was in peril. His activities had been too inconspicuous to merit the dignity of official notice of any kind. He had faithfully followed his foot-sore round of minor police courts, hospitals, one-alarm fires, and dreary public meetings, to have his copy jammed as scanty paragraphs under the head of "City Jottings." A "story" filling a third of a column had marked his one red-letter day on the *Standard*.

Each afternoon, at one o'clock, he hurried to his pigeon-hole in the row of letter-boxes by the city editor's door, his heart thumping to this sense of intangible fear, and with it pulsing the foolish hope of a "big assignment." Some day they must give him a chance, and he would show them whether or not he could handle something worth while. But the flame of hope was low on this dull day of June as Wilson unlocked his box and tore open the yellow envelope on which his name was scrawled.

He whistled in blank amazement as he followed an unfamiliar hand down to the managing editor's signature. The youngster's face flushed and his fingers twittered as he turned sharply to see if the loungers at their desks had noted his agitation. Then he stole into the hall and re-read, with his lips moving as if he were spelling out the words:

DEAR MR. WILSON: You have been pegging away without any let-up for three months and your work has been excellent. Here is an easy assignment as a reward of merit. It will give you a pleasant outing, and us a good page story for the Sunday sheet. The enclosed clipping from to-day's paper will give you the idea. The art department will have a snap-shot camera waiting for you. Our Ship-News man made arrangements this morning for you to be met and taken aboard. The one-forty train from Broad Street Station will take you through to Lewes and the Breakwater. To save time I enclose some expense money. Try to be back on Thursday. This will give you three days at sea. We want plenty of rattling description and human interest, with local color *ad lib*. Good luck.

"Oh, there must be some mistake," gasped young Wilson. "A page Sunday story? A whole page? My work has been excellent? The managing editor has been following it? Why, I didn't suppose he knew me by sight. I can't believe it."

Befogged with hopes and fears, he turned back to the door of the city editor's room.

"He's just gone out to lunch with the managing editor," volunteered the day assistant. "No, I don't know where they went. Said they'd be back about two-thirty."

Wilson looked at the office clock. If he would catch the one-forty train for Lewes there was no leeway for hesitation. He started toward the elevator, then halted to read the clipping, which might throw some light upon this staggering manifesto:

THE LAST PILOT SCHOONER

> The new steam pilot-boat will go into commission off the Delaware Capes early next week. This change from sail to steam is another blow at the romance of blue water. Six of the eight trim schooners of the Delaware fleet have already been dismantled, not only the *Albatross, Number One* is cruising on the station. She will be laid up as soon as the steamer is ready to put the pilots aboard incoming vessels. Every ocean voyager will regret the passing of the pilot schooner. These stormy petrels among sailing craft have been the first messengers from the looked-for land, as specks in the tumbling waste of sea, or lying hove to in all weathers....

Wilson threw his doubts overboard. All he had ever read of bellying canvas, whipping spars, and lee rails awash leaped into the foreground of his boyish imagination. Here was his chance for such a "descriptive story" as he had dreamed of through weeks and months, this last cruise of the last pilot schooner. He dashed into the art room, snatched up the waiting camera, and bolted for the station. After he dropped panting into a seat of the accommodation train for Lewes, he found himself already overhauling his stock of sea-lore and sailor adjectives.

There was time for reflection in this four-hour journey to the sea, and ere long, sober second thought began to overtake his first wild elation. The young reporter's doubts came trooping back. He remembered now that he had never written a line of "ship-news" for the *Standard*. He blushed to confess to himself that his life on salt water had been bounded by the decks of river excursion steamers. And what had he ever done worth the notice of the managing editor? Of course, he had worked hard, and the world, at least in fiction, occasionally rewarded honest merit in lowly places with unexpected largess. But any "star man" of the staff would have given a week's salary for such a note as this from the chief executive of the *Standard*. And he, James Arbuthnot Wilson, was indubitably the rawest and humblest recruit of that keen and rough-riding squadron of talent.

An inevitable reaction swung his mood into the forebodings. The train was loafing along the upper reaches of Delaware Bay when he re-read the intoxicating note, and caught himself repeating "Dear Mr. Wilson," with a sudden glimmer of association. In another miserable moment the youth's beautiful dream was wrenched from him. What a fool he had been! "Wilson," "Wilson," he muttered and burst out:

"Of course, there is another Wilson, the tip-top man of the staff. It's the Wilson who's been filling in as chief of the Washington Bureau for six months. I heard somebody say the other night that 'Doc' Wilson was coming back, and was to go on general work again. He must have turned up over Sunday. And that new boy put his note in my box. Well, I am IT."

Young James Arbuthnot Wilson squeezed back a smarting tear. He did not try to fence with this surmise. There was no room for doubt that the kind words and the pleasant outing had been aimed at his high-salaried elder. James Arbuthnot had never clapped eyes on the gifted "Doc" Wilson, whose Washington dispatches had carried no signature and whose distant personality had made no impression upon this wretched understudy of his.

How could the pilgrim muster courage to go back and face the issue? He would be the office butt—Well, he could resign, but most likely, he reflected, dismissal would be the instant penalty of this incredibly presumptuous blunder. The only thing to be done was to drop off at the next way station and return to the scene of his downfall. But to his stammering plea the brakeman returned:

"Next train up won't get along here till late to-night. You better go through to Lewes instead of waiting seven hours at one of these next-to-nothing flag stations."

The reporter slumped into his seat and looked through the open window. The tang of brine was in the breeze that gushed up the bay with the rising tide. Across the green fields he began to glimpse flashing blue water and bits of the traffic of far-off seas. A deep-laden tramp freighter was creeping toward her port, a battered bark surged solemnly in tow of an ocean-going tug, and a four-masted schooner was reaching up the bay with every sail pulling. Across the aisle of the car Wilson noticed, with a melancholy pleasure, four deep-tanned men of rugged aspect, who played cards with much talk of ships and tides and skippers. They belonged in this picture.

Wilson thought of the stewing city far behind him, and the spirit of some sea-faring ancestor was whispering in his ear. Yes, by Jove! he would see the tragic venture through after all. It were better to return with a "story," and fall with colors flying than to slink back to empty ridicule. Let them try to overtake him if they dared. This was "Mr. Wilson's" mission, and no one could snatch it from him.

When the train labored into Lewes, the fugitive looked across the flats to the cuddling arm of the Breakwater and the shining sea beyond. With the instinct of the hunted, he made ready to flee in this direction, away from the station and the town. As he dropped from the car, a man in the uniform of a station agent climbed aboard and shouted:

"Telegram for Mr. Wilson. Is Mr. Wilson aboard? Urgent telegram for Mr. J. A. Wilson."

Mr. Wilson's pulse fluttered as he dove behind the warehouse across the tracks, while the hoarse cry of the station agent rang horribly in his ears. The long arm of the *Standard* had almost clutched him by the collar. As he hurried down the nearest street to the water, he saw heading toward him a lusty youth of a sailorish cut, who eyed the camera case as if hasty suspicions were confirmed.

"Is your name Wilson?" demanded the stranger. "If it be, come along with me. I'm from the *Albatross'* boat-crew."

Wondering how much guilt was written in his face, Wilson fervently shook the hand of the briny youth. They fared toward the pier, while the convoy explained:

"You're in luck. We're ready to go to sea as soon as you get aboard. Hit it just right, didn't you? The pilots'll be glad to see you again. They was tickled to death over the piece you wrote for the paper when the *Eben Tunnell, Number Three*, come in after fightin' through the '88 blizzard, and specially what you wrote about ol' 'Pop' Markle stickin' by the *Morgan Castle* when she ketched fire off the Capes two year ago. And, say, they still talk about that jack-pot you sky-hooted clean through the cabin skylight, and how th' Pilots' Association went in mournin' for thirty days after that poker game. Two o' them boys is aboard this cruise, with the chips all stacked an' waitin', and their knives whetted. I'm sorry I missed the fun before."

James Arbuthnot Wilson gulped hard at these lamentable tidings. He was vaulting from the frying-pan into the fire. These rude and reckless men would probably heave him overboard. And, alas, the penny-ante of his mild college dissipations had left him as deficient in poker prowess as in sea-lore. The foremast hand from the *Albatross* was somewhat crestfallen over his capture. If this slip of a boy was the seasoned and capable "Doc" Wilson, able to hold his own in all weather and any company, then appearances were basely deceiving, and the escort felt a sense of personal grievance.

The boat was waiting at the pier and the four slouching seamen rowed out to the black schooner, which lazily rolled her gleaming sides off the end of the Breakwater. Wilson climbed awkwardly aboard and was saved from sprawling his length on deck by a strong hand, which yanked him in a welcoming grip. Then a stocky man with a grizzled mustache stepped back and fairly shouted:

"Why, hell! You ain't 'Doc' Wilson. What kind of a game is this? I popped up from below in time to see your hat coming over the side. Kick me, please. I'm dreamin', as sure as my name's McCall."

He fished a rumpled telegram from his blue clothes, and flourished it before the nose of his guest, as he cried formidably:

"Read that!"

"'Doc' Wilson, of the *Standard*, will be down on afternoon train. Take him aboard and treat him right."

Young Wilson looked at the half mile of water between the schooner and the beach, and thought of trying to swim for it. But the bully-ragging tone of the pilot struck a spark of his latent pluck and he answered with some spirit:

"I'm mighty sorry you're so disappointed. My name is Wilson, James Arbuthnot Wilson, of the *Standard*. The order to join your boat was delivered to me. If there's been a mistake, and I'm so unwelcome, I'll have to put you to the trouble of setting me ashore again."

The innate hospitality of his kind smothered the pilot's first emotions, and he regretted his rudeness as he smote the lad on the back and shouted:

"All right, Jimmy Arbutus. I guess there's no great damage done. It's now or never for your newspaper, and if we can't carry the skipper, we'll get along with the mate of your outfit. And we'll give you a cruise to make your lead-pencil smoke. Tumble below and shake them natty clothes. The boat-keeper will fit you out with a pair of boots and a jumper."

Sore and abashed, with the hateful emotions of an intruder, Wilson crept below and faced another ordeal. In the pilots' roomy cabin, which ran half the length of the schooner, four men were changing their clothes and tidying up their bunks. One of them emerged from the confusion to yell at the invader's patent leather ties:

"Hello, Doc, you old pirate. Is that you? Glad to see you aboard. Well, I will be damned!"

His jaw dropped and he looked sheepish as a hurricane voice came through the open skylight:

"Don't hurt the kid's feelin's. I've done plenty of that. This is Jimmy Arbutus Wilson, apprentice to 'Doc,' and he's doin' the best he can. 'Doc' got stranded somewheres, and the lad is takin' his run. I don't fathom it a little bit, but what's the odds?"

The passenger was introduced to all hands, who showed a depressing lack of enthusiasm, and the pilots returned to their tasks. Wilson retired, blushing and confused, to the edge of his bunk. Presently the oldest man of the party sat down beside the intruder, and shook his hand for the second time. Wilson raised his downcast face to the white-haired veteran, who said softly:

"Now, sonny, don't let the boys rile you none. They're kinder sore on some of the greenhorns that writes pieces all wrong for the Philadelphy papers, and this 'Doc' Wilson knows sailor ways and sailor lingo, and they sorter took a shine to him and his style. But fur's I know, you can write rings around him. And Old Pop Markle, as they calls me, will see you through, blow high, blow low. It's my last cruise, this is. I'm past seventy year, sonny, and my oldest boy is a pilot; he brought a tanker in yestiddy, and my grandson is servin' his apprentice years, and he'll be gettin' his papers pretty soon. It's time for me to quit. I was goin' to lay up ashore in the spring, but I kinder wanted to wind up with the old *Albatross*. Better come on deck, sonny; we're shortenin' cable."

Wilson smiled his gratitude at the gentle and garrulous old pilot, whose smooth-shaven face was webbed with fine-drawn wrinkles, as if each salty cruise had left its own recording line. The blue eyes were faded from staring into fifty years of sun and wind, but they held a beaming interest in the welfare of this tyro struggling in the meshes of hostile circumstance.

The reporter followed his guardian on deck, and his spirits swiftly rose. The *Albatross* was paying off under a flattened forestaysail, while her crew tailed onto the main-sheet with a roaring chorus, for they, too, felt a thrill of sentiment in this last cruise. The wind held fresh from the south'ard, and under the smooth lee of Cape Henlopen the *Albatross* shot seaward, as if they were skating over a polished floor. Now the pilots came tumbling up, and shouted as they turned to and helped set the maintopsail and staysail. The schooner staggered down to it, until the white water hissed over her low bulwark, and sobbed through the scuppers. "Old Pop" Markle slapped his knee and cried huskily:

"Give her all she'll stand, boys. It's like old times when we raced that dodgasted *Number Four* and hung to the weather riggin' by our teeth, and bent a new suit of sails every other cruise."

Holding the wind abeam, the *Albatross* drove straight out to sea, and then, once clear of Cape May, slid off to the north'ard. Now, the quartering sea picked her up and she swooped down the slopes and tried nimbly to climb the frothing hills, as the jolly wind smote her press of canvas and jammed her smoking through them. A new exhilaration surged in young Wilson's veins. He was drinking it all in, the buoyant flight of the low, slim schooner, the intimate nearness of the sea, the sweetness of the wind, and the solemnity of the marching twilight. He would not have been elsewhere for worlds. Then the fat and sweating face of the cook appeared from below, and bellowed an inarticulate summons.

The pilots obeyed with ardor, and Wilson followed timidly in their wake. Supper smoked on the cabin table, and the guest was glad to survey the stout fare of hash, cold meat, potatoes, green peas, flaky hot biscuits, and a mammoth pudding. "Old Pop" Markle took the youngster under his protecting wing, and found a seat on the locker beside his own. The reporter fell to, while the pilots chatted with bursts of gusty laughter. He made one desperate rally to join the talk, and in a quiet moment asked a neighbor:

"How do you know when a ship wants a pilot?"

"We generally have a trained green parrot that flies over and asks 'em," was the cruel response. "But we ran short of stores last cruise, and had to eat him. This voyage we intend to mail 'em postal cards."

There was an appreciative roar, and Wilson winced as "Old Pop" Markle whispered:

"Don't mind that Peter Haines. He's got a heart as soft as mush. It's only their skylarkin', sonny. Hit 'em back. That's what they like."

But the victim had lost all self-confidence, and now he was beginning to feel dizzy and forlorn. The smell of food, the heat, and the jerky plunging of the cabin were overwhelming. He staggered to his bunk and crept in. This was the last blow, that on top of his false pretences he should be laid low before the eyes of this hostile crowd. He knew not what happened, until hours after he awoke from a semi-stupor to find "Old Pop" Markle sponging his face with cold water and calling in his ear:

"There's a steamer coming up from the east'ard. Brace up and get on deck. It's a pretty sight."

The boy clambered through the companionway as the boat-keeper touched a match to an oil-soaked bunch of waste in a wire cage at the end of his torch. The schooner and the near-by sea were bathed in a yellow glare. Out in the darkness a blue Coston light glowed a response. Some one shouted: "On deck for the skiff," and five minutes later the boat-crew was pulling off in the night to the waiting steamer, with a pilot in the stern-sheets.

"There goes your friend, Peter Haines," chuckled "Pop" Markle. "I knowed you'd take it hard if I didn't give you a chance to say good-bye to him. He won't pester you no more this cruise."

The wind blew some of the cobwebs from poor Wilson's muddled head, and he felt refreshed. Soon the pelting spray drove him below deck and he curled up on a locker, watching the poker game from which youth and inexperience barred him. And what was more cutting, he was not even asked to play.

"It would be like taking pennies from a blind child," callously commented the strapping McCall who had welcomed him aboard. But the white-haired patriarch of them all did not join the game, and he said cheerily to Wilson:

"You're too young and I'm too old to be wastin' our wages in them pursuits, ain't we, sonny? There's an old lady and a cottage at Lewes that takes care of my rake-off. And instid of raisin' the limit, I raise vegetubbles for my fun."

Wilson opened his bruised heart and told the old pilot the story of his venture, and felt relieved that his masquerade had been thrown away. "Pop" Markle's blue eyes twinkled:

"See here, Jimmy Arbutus, I'll see that you write a fust-rate piece for your paper. Ask me anything your amazin' ignorance tells you to. The boys wanted me to take in the fust vessel we met, and was willin' to shove their turns aside, but I told 'em it was my last cruise, and I was goin' to see her through to the finish. So we've lots of time to talk pilotin' together. What was the most remarkable experience ever I had? Pshaw, that sounds like a full-rigged reporter, sonny, really it does.

"Well, I never got drownded boardin' a vessel, but I once fell afoul of a skipper that was a worse blunderin' idjit than you've been. It may sound kinder comfortin' to you. About fifty miles off the Capes, I clumb aboard an Italian bark. Her captain said he was bound for Wilmington, and would I take him in? He got a tow-boat at the Breakwater, and we were goin' up the river all right, when plumb by accident this benighted Dago imparted to me that he was bound for Wilmington, North Caroliny. 'Great Scott! You dodgasted lunatic,' says I, 'you're pretty nigh up to Wilmington, Delaware.' He went crazier than ever, and put about for sea after I showed him on the chart where he was at. He had been runnin' by dead-reckonin', and didn't know where he was. So, when he picked up a pilot and found he was headed all right for Wilmington, he figured his troubles were over. So there's worse than you afloat, Jimmy Arbutus."

At his suggestion, Wilson dug up his notebook and scribbled therein many other yarns, for the old pilot warmed to his task, and insisted that each of the poker players should contribute a story to the fund. When he was routed out for breakfast, the party had lost another pilot who had found his ship at daybreak. The wind had drawn into the northeast, and the *Albatross* was snuggled down under double reefs. The barometer was falling, and the boat-keeper shook his head when the pilots insisted upon edging further off shore.

"Drive her till she cracks," shouted McCall. "This is the trip when we keep going till we get our ships. The *Albatross* goes home empty, you bet your boots."

With much daring and difficulty one man was put aboard a liner late in the afternoon. Three pilots were left, and they swept Wilson into their genial comradeship, as the little party clawed its way to supper, and hung onto the table by its eyelids. In his mind, Wilson began to see the page story, "full of human interest and color." To-morrow he would work at his "introduction," and the thought of really making a start at filling those stately columns was perturbing. He felt something like stage-fright at the notion of it.

Before midnight, James Arbuthnot Wilson had forgotten his "story," and was thinking only of the awful turmoil above him. The wind had leaped to the might of a sudden summer gale. The schooner was hove to and battened tight, and like a tightly corked bottle she danced over the shouting seas. Made sick and giddy, Wilson sought "Old Pop" Markle, who was peacefully snoring in the next bunk, and shook him awake.

"Pshaw, sonny," the old man muttered, "she's safer than a big ship. She'll rare and tear and sputter till it blows over. If it'll ease your mind any, I'll take a peek on deck."

The pilot slipped into his oil-skins and vanished.

"It's pretty thick," he said when he came below, "but there ain't no great sea on, not for us. Rainin' hard and blowin' some. McCall is standin' watch with the boat-keeper. You're safer than if you was in the *Standard* office. You can't lose your job out here, Jimmy."

Somewhat comforted, Wilson tried to sleep. It was a terrifying experience for the greenhorn, with more "local color" than he had bargained for. Some time later in the night he was half dreaming that "Doc" Wilson was holding his head under water and drowning him with the most enjoyable deliberation.

With a crashing sound like the explosion of a great gun in his ears, he was flung headlong clear across the cabin, and on top of him came "Old Pop" Markle, sputtering harmless curses. The cabin floor sloped like the side of a house and stayed there as Wilson scrambled to his hands and knees. Then came a more sickening lurch, and before the hanging cabin lamp was smashed against the deck-beams, the lad saw that the old man was dazed. He gave him a hand, and together they climbed the slope, and grasped the legs of the stationary table. They heard the other pilots stumble up the companion ladder, and hammer back the hatch, with yells of terror lest they be trapped.

Forward of the cabin bulkhead, they heard the roar of inrushing water, and smothered outcries among the watch below. While the old man and the boy tried to grope their way aft to the ladder, the sea crashed through the bulkhead door from the galley beyond, and instantly they were picked up and hurled aft, choking and fighting for life. Wilson chanced to grasp a step of the ladder, and with his free arm pulled "Old Pop" Markle to this refuge. The reporter did not want to die, and he knew that death dragged him by the heels. And it was with no heroic prompting that he pushed the old man up ahead of him. It was done on the instant, as one friend would help another in a pinch, without wrought-out purpose.

The water was sucking at his waist as he fought his way up, and partly out, and managed to double himself over the hatch coaming, with the old man's legs across his shoulders. Thus they were half jammed in the cramped exit. Just then the flare torch was lighted by a seaman. In the yellow glare "Old Pop" Markle saw the two pilots and two, only two, of the crew wrestling with the one skiff left at the davits. One of them stopped to beckon wildly to the old man and started to go to his aid.

In this moment the schooner lurched under with a weary, lifeless roll, and a black sea stamped across her sodden hull. It licked up the boat and the handful of toiling men, it leaped forward and pulled down the black figure with the torch. The two men still jammed in the hatchway were cruelly battered, but they could not be wrenched away. And when the towering comber had passed, there was darkness and silence, and no more shouting voices on the schooner's deck.

The old pilot wriggled free and got his hands on a life-buoy that hung within his reach at the after end of the cabin hatch. Wilson dragged himself after him, and pitched against a splintered mass of planking upended against the wheel. They listened and heard a steamer's imploring whistle, and one faint cry off to leeward. "Pop" Markle groaned as he fumbled in the darkness and laboriously passed a tangle of line around the wreck of the skylight cover to which Wilson was clinging.

"Hang on, sonny," he gasped. "I've made the buoy fast to the loose timber. We'll go off together with the next sea, sure. My God! here it comes."

The dying schooner seemed to sink from beneath them, and clinging to their frail bit of a raft, they were spun off to leeward in the arms of the sea that swamped the rock-ballasted *Albatross*. Turned over and over, the two men fought for breath until the skylight cover righted, and they came to the surface. They slid swiftly into a murky hollow, and were borne to the tattered crest whose froth was strangling.

But the wind was falling fast. Such seas as those which had broken over the helpless *Albatross* were running in swollen billows when they met no barrier to check them. Therefore the castaways could cling and breathe, and even made shift to pass the loose ends of the line around their waists while they waited for the end. Now their spray-blinded eyes dimly saw the lights of the steamer that had bitten halfway through the pilot-schooner. She was blundering far to windward, and her signal rockets cut red gashes in the night. They could watch her swing in a useless circle as she sought to find the craft she had struck. Drifting away to leeward, the old pilot and the young reporter tried to shout, but their little rasping cries were pitifully futile. They coughed the racking brine from their throats, and saw the last rocket soar, saw the steamer's lights fade in the rain, become twinkling points and vanish.

*The last of the "Albatross."*

There were no words between them until the day began to break. Now and then one sought the other's hand and found a feebly responsive grip. Thus they knew that death had not come to the little raft. With the gray light, the wind veered round to the south'ard, and except for the swinging swell, the sea was smoothed to summer gentleness. The eternal miracle of dawn had never come to more grateful hearts than these two. Youth had survived the battering ordeal with mind still alert, but old age was near passing with hurts and exhaustion. Now that he could see no help, the boy so managed it that the pilot could lie half across the life-buoy, which floated high with the supporting planking beneath it.

"Them as wasn't drownded and smashed in their bunks, couldn't swim, or none to speak of," sighed the old man. "I knew 'em all from boys. Two left.... And we're the most wuthless of the lot, sonny. But you may learn how to make an honest livin' some day.... Don't bother with me.... I'm due to go.... The old lady has the cottage, and there's the pension from the Pilot's Fund.... And two more pilots in the family.... Ain't you sorry you didn't let 'Doc' Wilson come?"

The boy sputtered:

"No, we aren't dead yet, and if we're picked up it's the story of a lifetime. I don't believe the Lord saved us from the wreck to die on a summer morning like this. And, my, but you were good to me, Mr. Markle."

They floated in silence while the June sun rose higher, and heat and thirst piled up their wretchedness. The seasoned fiber of the old man had been toughened for such a stress as this. He hung on grimly because he had always hung on grimly to whatever life set him to endure. Although they were out on the edge of traffic bound in and out of the Delaware Capes, he still hoped, but mostly for the boy.

Six hours after the *Albatross* had gone to the bottom, a boat from a crippled brig, laden with salt from Turk's Island, picked up a bit of wreckage to which were lashed a white-haired man and a beardless lad. Both were too weak to talk, and the British skipper had them put into bunks, and poured raw Jamaica rum down their throats. Wilson was the first to revive, but he could not rise, and had to content himself with tidings that the pilot was alive and conscious. Night had come before the reporter could totter as far as the mate's cabin and see his comrade.

The pilot's leathery face was strangely bleached, and he could no more than whisper with a faltering huskiness:

"God bless their poor souls. They was all neighbors of mine. Hello, Jimmy Arbutus, have you begun to write that piece for the paper? There's something wrong with my insides. I think I busted some of 'em when we was jammed in that hatch. Well, we're going home, my son. Are you all taut again?"

Wilson tried to hide his anxiety and set himself to nursing the old man as best he could. His clumsy attentions were received with a sweet resignation, but the old man showed signs of impatience. At length, unable to restrain his desire, he asked:

"Why don't you begin to write your piece instead of wastin' time on my old hulk? I want to see it's done all ship-shape. We ain't goin' to have no 'Doc' Wilson nor a lot of fresh young pilots laughin' at our blunders. I'll overhaul the writin' for you."

Wilson was eager to begin. The skipper found a half-filled log-book, and the butt of a pencil, and the reporter sat by the pilot's bunk, and wrote with frowning effort. His labor was so evident that at length the interested pilot asked:

"You seem to be making heavy weather of it, Jimmy. Mind my lookin' over the nigh end of it?"

Wilson passed the log-book over with a flutter of expectancy. He was proud of his opening paragraphs. He flattered himself that he had caught the spirit of the tragedy of the last and lost pilot-schooner. The old man read them with puckered brow, and laid the book down without comment. Wilson waited and had to break the awkward silence:

"Anything the matter with that?"

"Well, I had only a common school education, and I've been at sea fifty years. I'm no judge, I guess. It's too high-falutin' for me. Those dictionary words are mighty imposin', and the opening verse of poetry looks gilt-edged. But, well, every man to his trade."

The very young reporter looked hurt, and the pilot tried to soothe him by flatly denying the truth of everything he had said. Wilson put the book away and went on deck. In his mind there was a glimmering notion that his literary method might be open to criticism. The old fear and lack of self-confidence came back. He would rest another day and try again.

Next morning the brig was beating against a baffling wind, and the Delaware Capes were two hundred and fifty miles away. A mattress was brought on deck, and the old man was laid on it beneath an awning. He was growing weaker, and began to fret when he found the brig was making so little headway toward her port and his home. Wilson was moody and worried about his comrade. He had no heart for his "story."

After a while the British skipper sat down beside the old man, and began to ask him about the loss of the *Albatross*. The pilot began with the start of the last cruise, and with crisp and homely detail, and with many breaks in his voice, he carried the tale down to the loss of the vessel, the loss of his comrades, and the escape of the oldest and youngest of those that had sailed in her. And because he felt it all so deeply, the story did not once wander from its chartered course.

Wilson pulled himself together and picked up his log-book. He felt that it was his duty to write what he heard. When he had finished, the scales fell from his eyes, for at a great price he had been taught to discern that virtue of simplicity which most of his craft must spend years to learn. When the pilot fell into a doze, he stole below and began to write his "story." It was not all as the pilot had told it, but its backbone and its vitals belonged to the simple and untutored old man. Next day when he read it to "Pop" Markle the pilot brightened and observed:

"Any sailor could understand that, my lad. It sounds as dodgasted ordinary as if I had wrote it myself. The pilots will think a heap of that piece. I want you to hold your job, sonny."

The third day passed, and then the fourth, and the booming head wind was holding the lubberly brig out of sight of the Delaware Capes. The pilot insisted that he be carried on deck whenever the sun shone. He was looking for the Henlopen light. When he was not drowsy, he would talk of home to his young comrade, for all his thoughts were flocking thither.

"I don't think I'm going to fetch it, sonny," he murmured when the fifth day broke with no land in sight. "It looks like you're going to be the sole survivor of the *Albatross*. That will make your piece a heap stronger, won't it? My own boy couldn't have done more for me than you have. If we don't pick up the Capes by noon, I want you to write a letter for me to Mary, that's my wife. You can take it ashore at Lewes. You'll find the cottage easy enough. And you must go around and look at my vegetubbles. One of my boys will be home, and he'll see that they get my hulk to the buryin' ground. The skipper here has promised to anchor long enough to send me ashore."

Wilson choked, and tried to cheer the old man. But the faded blue eyes were serene with the foreknowledge of his end. The letter was written at his dictation, and Wilson sobbed while he went below to find an envelope in the skipper's desk. Then the pilot tried to sign it, and his knotted brown fingers held the pencil while Wilson helped him trace the wavering:

"Your loving Seth."

Late in the afternoon of this, the fifth day, a tiny shaft, like a beckoning finger, cut the cloudless western skyline. Seth Markle heard the shouts of the men clustered forward who were eager to bring him the longed-for news. Wilson and the skipper came to him, and propped him up in his pillows on the poop-deck.

"Henlopen light," he whispered. "Henlopen light, and Lewes just around the Point."

The dim light of life burned brighter in this draught of hope, but soon waned lower than before. After a long silence, the old man tried to speak. Wilson put his ear close to the resolute mouth, and could barely hear:

"Tell her how good you've been to me. I—I hope the piece is all right. The last cruise.... Oh, Mary, you're waiting around the Point of the Cape."

He was alive until sunset, but he did not speak, except once when Wilson thought he heard a fluttering whisper of "Mary," and after that the rough-hewn face became very peaceful.

The brig crept into the lee of the Breakwater soon after daylight next morning. Wilson went ashore and found the cottage with the marvelous vegetable garden, and a sweet-faced woman who read her letter while the bearer walked softly among the cabbage rows, and noted, with a quick pang, how lovingly they had been tended. Presently Mary Markle came to him, and put her motherly arms around his neck and kissed him through her tears. They went to a near-by cottage where dwelt the eldest son. There Wilson left them. Before he went away he said:

"He was the best friend I ever had. I'm coming down day after to-morrow. May I go to the church with you?"

He had to tarry in the streets, for the news had spread, and other weeping wives of pilots and seamen pressed around him. When, as tenderly as possible, he was able to leave them, he went to the telegraph office and sent this message to the managing editor of the *Standard*:

"Just landed. Am sole survivor of pilot schooner *Albatross* run down and foundered a week ago. Will report with my story at noon."

On the train Wilson added to his "story" in the old log-book the facts of the last days of Pilot Seth Markle. His pencil quivered and balked when he recalled the words and face of his gentle old critic, and somehow, through his tears, he brought the narrative of the last cruise to its unadorned conclusion. Then he closed the book and leaned back with a great weariness. Now he was passing that bright vista of shore through which he had first seen the Bay, where he had chosen to advance rather than to retreat. Those intervening days seemed like years of life. He had gone away a boy, he was coming back a man.

When the young reporter walked into the *Standard* office, the first man to greet him was a bald and bulky stranger with an impressive manner, who said:

"Ah, the young hero, I presume. You had a great streak of luck, didn't you? Glad to see you pulled through. My name is Wilson. I'm to take your notes at once and work up the story from them. We're going to play as the leading feature in to-morrow's paper, and follow up with a page for Sunday."

Young Wilson looked at "Doc" Wilson with a new assertiveness and threw back his slight shoulders as he replied:

"No, thank you. Nothing doing. My story is written, and it's going to be turned in to the boss as it stands. I'm going in to see him now."

"Oh, nonsense," snapped "Doc" Wilson. "I can understand your wanting to do the story, and your head being swelled a bit and all that. But if you want to hold your job you'd better fork over your notes without any more fuss about it. The old man passed it out that he was going to fire you, anyhow. I'll say a good word for you if you can produce the goods."

Young Wilson brushed past his elder, who stood dumbfounded at the insolence of the "pup." Then the managing editor was confronted by an unabashed intruder, who announced:

"Here's my story, sir. There's about six columns of it. And it's all ready to be edited. And no 'Doc' Wilson nor anybody else is going to rewrite it until you've passed on it."

The managing editor saw a bedraggled figure with a firm-set jaw and a level glance which looked him squarely in the eyes. He took in the sea-stained clothes, and the burned and grimy face, and smiled as he said:

"I'll read it, Mr. Wilson. Go home and come back at six o'clock. Then we'll talk it over. You've been through a tremendous experience, haven't you? It's your story. Don't fret about that."

When James Arbuthnot Wilson next entered the managing editor's office, that dignified personage grasped his hand and exclaimed:

"My son, why haven't I known you could write a story like this? It's the real thing. It's a masterpiece. Where did you learn how?"

The boy's face twitched as he said very slowly:

"The man who taught me how died in sight of home. It's his story. It isn't mine at all. I want a day off, if you please, to go down to Lewes again. I'm—I'm the last of the *Albatross*."

# THE JADE TEAPOT

Private Saunders, of the Ninth Infantry, was flushed and dazed with fever, but able to walk from the ambulance up a stone stairway into what looked to him like a huge and gilded warehouse. At first glance, he did not see the long rows of cots whose gray blankets blended with the carpet of dusk and shadow in the late winter afternoon. Monstrous golden dragons seemed to writhe and flicker against the roof beams far above him, or twist in play on lines of massive columns. Saunders dropped his kit and leaned on his rifle while he rubbed his eyes with a trembling hand. If this was the hospital of the American army in Peking, he wished that some one would turn out the guard and capture the menagerie that had taken possession. Sliding uncertain feet across the flagged floor, he fell over a cot and gripped a protesting leg, whose owner sputtered:

"Get off o' me, you left-footed lobster. Ain't there no chance for a man to be sick without the roof fallin' on him? Why, hello, Jim, what in blazes is the matter with you? Brace up and holler for the orderly. He's somewhere down at the end of the line, packin' up what's left of Chase of P Company, who just passed in his checks."

Saunders sat on the edge of the cot and wept with the whimper of a tired child:

"Is it the hospital sure enough, Shorty? All them ten-foot dragons makin' faces at me in the dark ain't comfortin' to a man with wheels in his head. Guess this must be the Emp'ror's private temple. Why, here's a dozen o' my pals spraddled around over the floor. I've hit the right place, all right. Lead me to my bunk, an' get me bedded down."

The overworked hospital corps private, who was nurse and orderly for the ward, picked up the accouterments of Saunders, and helped him crawl under the blankets of the cot alongside "Shorty" Blake. The contract surgeon, delaying to question a group of convalescents in the courtyard, came in to examine the new patient, and said "pneumonia" to the nurse. Saunders heard nothing of the consultation, for he was looking up into the gloom of the distant rafters, and trying to count the racing gilded dragons that would not be still and made his head ache intolerably. When lanterns were lighted at the ends of each aisle, the shadows danced worse than before, and to his fevered eyes the great temple was populous with glittering shapes in terrifying agitation.

This, the largest of the clustered buildings in the park of the Temple of Earth, was an extraordinary hospital, even in daylight. Sacred to the annual pilgrimage of the Emperor in his worship of the Supreme Deity, these temples had been inviolate for many centuries until profaned by the conquering foreign allies. The walled park became the camp of the American forces, and one of the most sacred shrines of the land was used as a field hospital. A regiment could have been drilled on the marble pavement without crowding, and the two hundred sick soldiers scattered in the vastness of it were bitten with a sense of chilling desolation.

Between flights of delirium, through his first night in hospital, Saunders heard the groans and restless muttering of many men, and his fancies magnified them into an army. There were neither screens nor walls to divide the wards, only the rows of cots between the carved pillars that marched across the temple floor, so that all individual suffering and the tenacious struggle of dying became common property. The soldiers who passed away in the night time did not trouble their comrades so much as when death came in daylight, and the end was a spectacle thrust upon those in surrounding cots.

A little after midnight the tramp of stretcher bearers punctuated a thin and wailing outcry, coming from that which they bore, and the temple floor awoke with weary curses. Those near the doorway learned that a Chinese coolie, caught in the act of stealing coal from the quartermaster's corral, had been tumbled off a wall by a sentry's shot. The lamentations of the victim rasped sick nerves beyond endurance, and the hospital held no sympathy in its smallest crevice. The coolie was an old man and badly hurt. Opium had made him impervious to customary doses of morphine, and after he had been drugged in quantities to kill four men, he was no nearer rest. From a far corner of the temple the wounded coolie wailed an unending

"Ay oh"—"Ay oh"—"Ay oh!"

Soldiers rose in their blankets and made uproar with cries of—

"Kill him!"

"Smother the brute!"

"Give him an overdose!"

"Now, ain't this an outrage!"

"Hi, there, One Lung, give us a rest, for God's sake!"

"Throw him out in the yard."

Daylight brought to Saunders infinitely grateful respite from a world through which he had fled from flaming dragons that shrieked, as if in torture:

"Ay oh"—"Ay oh"—"Ay oh!"

The grip of his delirium weakened in a few days, and the surgeon called him a "mild case." At the end of a week, Saunders was able to sit up a little and talk with the men around him. But the violence of these early impressions in hospital had unstrung a system drained by long service in the Philippines, and by the contrasting hardships of the cold winter in North China. The gloomy temple frightened the soldier, for sometimes the private has nerves, but he kept his fears to himself, thinking them womanish. He fell to brooding too much of home, and the more he dwelt upon the distance between Peking and those who loved him the more insistent became his morbid fear that he would not go back with his company.

It happened almost daily that the Ninth Regiment band trailed through the hospital compound, playing a dead march. There was always a halt in front of the stone stairway, and after a few moments the dragging music sounded fainter and farther away. A little later those in the temple could barely hear the silvery wail of "taps" floating from a corner of the outer wall, where a line of mounds was growing longer week by week. Then the band returned, playing a Sousa march or a "rag-time" medley. The listeners in hospital filled in the gaps between the music, and the mind of Saunders was busiest of them all in picturing the routine of a soldier's funeral in Peking.

The surgeons looked him over in morning inspection rounds, and said there was nothing the matter to prevent his recovery. "Shorty" Blake and "Bat" Jenkins of P Company strove to make Saunders take some interest in life, and would have been cheered if he had even sworn at the rations and the lack of hospital comforts. They brought him jam and condensed milk from the commissary-sergeant, which he refused to eat; they assembled around his cot the most vivacious convalescents, selecting as entertainers those valiant in poker and campaign stories. Finally Saunders was persuaded to overhaul his haversack and show his slender store of souvenirs gathered in Peking. Blake and Jenkins moved over to pass opinion on the riches, and Saunders welcomed them tremulously:

"I was plannin' to take some things home to mother and sister," he began, "but I didn't have a chance to get much while the lootin' was busy. Wouldn't have done me any good if I had, when the captain had the tents searched and collared most of the company stuff. I ain't sorry I missed it on the loot, for the old lady 'ud throw out o' the window all the stuff I sent her, if she thought it wasn't paid for. She's fierce in backin' foreign missions, an' the Chinamen is her purticuler pets."

Shorty broke in with an oath: "Yes, I know all about P Company's captain and his hair-trigger conscience. He swiped all our loot, but he sent home forty-seven mail packages, duty free. I got that from the postal clerk. What you got left, Saunders?"

The invalid spread an embroidered panel of crimson satin and a roll of blue silk on the edge of his cot, and threw a handful of silver ornaments and a cloisonné snuff-box on the blankets.

"I didn't loot even this stuff," he said, with an apologetic air, "but bought it along the Chien-men Road, so it could go to the home folks with a clean bill of ladin'."

The spectators sniffed incredulously, but with unexpected tact hid any livelier display of doubt.

"Why don't you mail the goods home with a letter, and send a good jolly?" said Jenkins. "We'll get 'em off for you. There's a mail wagon goin' to Tientsin early to-morrow mornin'. Tell the old lady you're fat an' sassy. She'll call in the whole village to show 'em the presents from her brave soldier boy out among them poor, benighted, gentle, murderous Chinese heathen."

Saunders rallied for the afternoon, scrawled a letter, and sent his gifts. Then he buried his head in the blankets and wept, the effort having stirred new depths of hopeless homesickness. Through the following week he failed to gain in strength and spirits, and the surgeon mentioned "nostalgia" once or twice in chatting with the nurse.

"He may lie there and flutter out, with no disease worth a diagnosis," said the "medico." "The poor idiot thinks he would die on the way if he was shipped across country to Taku, to connect with a transport; and he's sure he'll be buried if he stays here. If we can get a little strength in him, I'll see what I can do to get him started home."

Saunders was not yet a dying man, but the natural process of recovery seemed at a standstill. There came a sharp turn for the worse after "Shorty" Blake limped in with a letter, which he tossed to the languid private with a cheery shout of—

"Wake up, Jim; here's the latest news from home. Hurry and tell us the price of butter an' eggs at the corner store."

But Saunders read the letter in silence, and while he read, his thin young face twitched, tears came, and the helpless length of him moved in little jerks that rippled the blankets.

The chaffing queries of his comrades were unanswered, and the patient seemed to be asleep through the afternoon and evening. When the light of the next morning filtered through the latticed windows of oiled paper, "Shorty" Blake saw Saunders grope for the letter under the blanket roll that served him for a pillow, and read it again. His voice was weaker than before, as he beckoned Blake and Jenkins to the cot, and said:

"Here's what comes of my leavin' home to be buried in this muck-heap of a town—an' my folks turned out to starve. You might as well read it, though you can't do any good."

Shorty saw a woman's handwriting, and he took the closely written sheets with singular gentleness. The spelling was imperfect in spots, and there were many erasures, but he stumbled through the uncertain lines, which said:

"MY DEAREST SON—

> "No letter has come from you since you left the Philippines, but I'm sure you are all right, because no notice has come to me from the War Department as your next of kin. All I know is that your regiment is in Peking, and I hope and pray you are with it, all safe and sound. Sister Mary and me are pretty busy, as there has been no one to help us with the place since your brother died last spring. I know your enlistment ain't up for another year, and it's wicked to desert, and they would shoot you for it anyhow, and whom the Lord loveth He chasteneth; but it does seem kind of hard when we want you so much at home that you have to be fighting them poor Chinamen when I've been sending money for their souls these thirty-seven years. But as long as we all have our health there ain't any real troubles I suppose.
> 
> "I don't mean to find fault and you mustn't worry about us. I'm as active as a cricket and Mary hasn't been ailin' any to speak of. It's been a good long spell of dry weather, and that's good for my rheumatism, but it wasn't very encouraging for the crops. The mortgage on the house and farm is due in six weeks, and I can't get a renewal, though it's only six hundred dollars, as you know. The bank people is that haughty about the thing that I don't exactly see how we can get around them.
> 
> "But where there's a will there's a way, and the Lord tempers the wind to the shorn lamb, and if we ain't got any cash, there's others worse off. Your uncle Joseph is breakin' up fast, and he's ten years younger

than me. He's the last of the tribe that's left on either side, and his family won't have anything to spare when he's gone. Of course it's hard to think of losing our old place, but I'm still pretty spry, and my black silk is good as new. I can't just quite tell where Mary and me will be if we leave home so soon, but you write just the same and the postmaster will know. You remember him, that stumpy, light-haired Jameson that married one of the Martins.

"God bless you, my poor wandering boy.

   Your loving

            "Mother."

Jenkins was reading over "Shorty's" shoulder, and several hairy faces framed in gray blankets had edged silently nearer.

"Well, what do you think of that?" said a Sixth Cavalry corporal. "And here's Saunders been givin' up the ghost without havin' any real troubles. Now it's time for you to brace up, and beg, borrow, or steal the dough and shoot it along to the old homestead. That letter was written more'n a month ago."

But Saunders had turned his face away and was a useless member of the ways and means committee, which convened with "Shorty" Blake as chairman. A praise-worthy burst of philanthropic ardor subsided when it met the cold fact that the paymaster had not visited camp in two months, and was not expected in Peking before three weeks later. Investigation revealed also that nearly all the available cash in P Company had passed into the hands of three expert poker players, who were reported as being "hard as nails, and wouldn't give a dollar to save their own mothers from the poorhouse."

Saunders showed no symptoms of interest in these endeavors, largely because he foresaw their magnificent futility. He was in a condition of hopeless apathy, and beyond rereading the letter from home now and then, made no effort to rally. He kept a tally of the days remaining before the foreclosure of the mortgage, with a series of thumb-nail scratches on the frame of his cot.

There were twelve days to be marked off when "Shorty" Blake, who had been discharged as cured, clattered into the ward, and yelled as he leaned over Saunders:

"I lost track of my dates while I was in this gold-plated asylum, and my discharge is due to-day, and I was figurin' my enlistment wasn't up for another week. There's a squad of discharged men goin' down to Tientsin in a wagon-train to-morrow, and I've drawn my travel pay, got my papers, and

I'm off for little old New York. Here's where I drop off on the way an' do what I can for your old folks in Kansas. Got anything you want to send them?"

Saunders became almost animated as he rolled over and tried to speak in a fluttering whisper:

"I ain't got any money for 'em; but tell 'em I was doin' well when you left me, and to keep their nerve, an' I'll get back as fast as I can. But speakin' between us, Shorty, there's nothin' doin' for me, and I'll be planted before you get to 'Frisco. Maybe I've got some little trick to send along. Wait a minute. Fish around under the cot and find me a roll of rubber blankets."

The uproarious "Shorty" opened the bundle and disclosed a jade teapot, in a wrapping of wadded silk. It was a flawless bit of carving, fashioned from a solid block of imperial green jade, no more than a pretty toy to the soldiers, who examined it indifferently and wondered why Saunders wished to send it to his mother.

"It's the last thing I've got," he explained, "and the last present they'll ever get from me. I think they'd like to know I wasn't so blamed forgetful at the finish. Just lug it along, Shorty, an' if it don't get broke on the way, you can mail it when you cross the country."

The wish and the token were a sick man's whim to Blake, but he wrapped the jade teapot and tucked it in a soft corner of his haversack when he packed his kit late that night. He was vaguely aware that his purpose of finding the distressed family of Saunders would not survive the journey home, yet he had meant it when he made the promise. He believed Saunders as good as dead, because he had seen men die of homesickness in the field hospitals of the Philippines.

"I'll send his silly teapot to his folks," he told another discharged private of P Company, as they climbed into a four-mule wagon next morning; "and I'm sorry I can't help him out, same as you are. If the doctor would pack the poor fool in a wagon and ship him to the sea, he couldn't any more than die on the way, and there 'd be a fightin' chance he'd brace up."

With this farewell tribute of sympathy, the fortunes of Private Saunders slipped into the background among the varied interests which occupied the attention of the late Private Blake along his route to Taku Bar.

In the hospital, Saunders continued to let go his grip on life as gently as possible. Tangible woe and regret had become active agents in assisting the passive manner of his fading away. A new major-surgeon came up from Tientsin to assume charge of the hospital, and he was angry when he examined Saunders and heard the history of the case. "That man is dying of homesickness and worry," he growled to the hospital corps private in the ward; "and now he hasn't enough vitality left in him to risk moving in an ambulance. He'd snuff out like a candle on the way to Tientsin, and you can't keep him alive more than two weeks longer. He may as well die in some comfort as be jolted to death."

Much of the time in the following week Saunders hovered along the borderland of dreams which were not wholly disquieting, for he had become on friendly terms with the gilded dragons on the shadowy rafters, and now and then they talked to him. The sick men of P Company had been sent back to duty, and Saunders did not know those who had taken their places along his aisle of the columned temple. When he noticed them, it was to whisper little inconsequential memories of home, and to tell passers-by of some new discovery gleaned from an intimate familiarity with numberless gilded dragons that never slept. He still noted the tally marks on the frame of his cot, and when he was too weak to reach them, the man in the nearest cot scratched a cross for him until only seven marks remained. The letter was no longer read, but the tragedy it told was woven through much of the delirious talk of the patient.

Meantime "Shorty" Blake had been routed with heavy loss among the canteens and other diversions of Tientsin, and, greatly the worse for wear, made his way to Taku and boarded a Japanese transport bound for Nagasaki. He went ashore in that entertaining port with three Mexican dollars as the melancholy remnant of his pay and travel allowance "to the place of enlistment," and presented his papers to the American quartermaster stationed in Nagasaki, who gave him an order for transportation on the next United States transport sailing for San Francisco.

Discharged Private Blake was much disconcerted when he was informed that no Government vessel was to stop en route from Manila in less than two weeks, and that he was stranded "on the beach," with several other recent losses to the fighting strength of the army in the Orient. A bundle of looted silk had been exchanged in Tientsin for bottles of astonishing Scotch whiskey made in Shanghai, and there was nothing else of cash value in the light marching order of ex-private Blake. He hired a room in a toy-like Japanese hotel, and late that night returned without his three Mexican dollars, but with the perverted energy of a runaway automobile. Charging headlong through the dainty paper walls of the hotel rather than be annoyed by trying to find the door mobilized a small army of Japanese policemen, and memory came back to Blake when he was dragged into the street, his haversack hurled at his head by the agitated landlord.

Daylight found him very thirsty and nervous, wandering along the edge of the bay, waiting for a glimpse of a blue army blouse and the tenuous hope of a small loan. He leaned against the stone wall of the Hatoba, with his haversack under his tortured head, and twisted as his cheek rubbed a hard lump beneath the canvas. Ramming his hand into the haversack with a peevish curse, "Shorty" pulled out a package wrapped in wadded silk, and unrolled a teapot of green imperial jade. A stocky manikin of the Nagasaki police was standing near, and the soldier addressed him and the sleeping harbor without partiality:

"If I didn't forget all about Jim Saunders and his teapot, I'm a liar. An' he must be dead an' planted by this time, an' the old homestead gone to hell, an' nothin' left but this looney little teapot as his last will an' testament. I'll surely send it to Kansas all right, tho' it ain't goin' to cheer the old lady very much. The teapot must be worth as much as a dollar and a half."

Then the demon of thirst gripped Blake by the throat, and the effort of swallowing fairly shook him. He slipped the teapot into his haversack, and to his credit it must be told that he struggled with temptation for several minutes. Then he muttered weakly: "I ain't goin' to sell it. The teapot will be all safe in hock till I can send for it or make a strike. Who's goin' to know the difference, anyway? Saunders had no business to pass away like a sick chicken, an' load me up with this billy-be-damned piece of bric-a-brac."

But shops and saloons were not yet opened, and "Shorty" Blake walked heavily along many blocks of silent streets, his thirst more raging and insistent as he found himself thwarted. Every scruple vanished and he was ready to sell the teapot for the price of a pint flask of anything searching and fiery.

The rattle of rickshaw wheels made him suddenly alert, and he stumbled toward the sound. As he turned a corner there was a collision, and the racing coolie in the shafts slid on his head, while the passenger barely saved himself from an ugly backward fall. The Japanese officer so nearly upset accepted the awkward apologies of the soldier derelict and politely asked whether he had been hurt. "Shorty" pulled himself together and, saluting instinctively, he spoke with breathless haste:

"No, sir, no damage done, and I hope you wer'n't shook up; but don't you want to buy a prime jade teapot, and help out an American soldier who's broke, an' ain't got no other means of support? I know it ain't worth much, bein' nothin' but a toy, but I need the price, whatever it is."

The officer bowed as if honored by the confidence, and replied: "It is not customary to sell jade teapots in the streets so early in the morning, and I am in the hurry to arrive with my duty. But Japan and America are so great friends since Peking, eh? Is it not? A-h, is th-a-a-t the jade, and from Peking, eh? I do not know everything about jade, but there are many good times for you in that teapot; ha, ha! I think so. I am not so mean to rob the honorable soldier. You will make a borrow of this two yen—two dollars—all right, eh? And you will take my card and the teapot will come with you at my house at noon hour, eh?"

Before the beclogged brain of "Shorty" Blake had caught up with these directions, the rickshaw was whisking around a curve of the hillside, and the derelict was left staring after, the jade teapot in one hand, and two one-yen notes in the other. Visions of wealth made him tingle, and he rewrapped the treasure with reverent deliberation. Then began another battle with a battered fragment of a conscience, and the voice of Saunders was so distinct in his ear that he turned suddenly more than once to mutter to the empty street:

"I'm on the edge of the shivers. It's a bad sign when you hear voices as plain as that. It's that baby whine of his, always cryin', 'Ten days more an' the folks will be homeless and starvin', an' I can't do nothin'.'

"Holy smoke! I've heard that string of dates often enough to keep track of 'em. An' there's three more days leeway or I've missed my count. An' me with a fortune in this little monkey-doodle teapot, if that Jap wasn't stringin' me."

From stories told later to his "bunkie" on the transport, it is probable that "Shorty" Blake passed through great mental stress during the forenoon of his second day in Nagasaki, but that this ordeal was nothing compared with his torments after an interview with a wealthy dealer in curios at the home of a major of Japanese infantry on the hill. There is reason to believe that the discharged private of the China Relief Expedition kept his appointment in a fairly sober condition, although much shaken and easily startled. An hour later, the Japanese officer accompanied "Shorty" Blake to the telegraph office and the branch of the Hong Kong and Shanghai Bank, with an air of anxious guardianship, as if determined to see a wavering project through to the finish. Shorty skipped references to his escort in subsequent narratives, as if the topic were painful, dismissing his interview with the sweeping summary:

"I had to go an' put that little Jap wise to the whole hard-luck story of Jim Saunders. Then he talked to me like a Dutch uncle, and had me on the mourners' bench in no time. Them Japs is strong on filial duty, and he never let up on me till the job was done."

Twenty-four hours later, the Signal Corps operator at the American army station in Peking copied a message addressed to "J. Saunders, P Company, Ninth Infantry, Field Hospital No. 1."

"Sold teapot for eight hundred dollars gold. Have cabled six hundred to old lady to bust mortgage. Will bust Nagasaki wide open with balance. If not dead, brace up.

(Signed)

"Shorty."

It seemed indecent to carry this telegram to the bedside of Private Saunders. He had lost all interest in the world of men and things, yet was inexplicably lingering, as if caught in an eddy as he drifted out. Fantasies had fled, and his mind was clearing, as if to pay some heed to the important business of ceasing to be. The message was first read by the major-surgeon, and there was more than professional interest in his tone, as he said to the nurse of the ward:

"Give that man ten drops of digitalis and a dose of brandy, and try to wake him up enough to understand this telegram. It's the only thing on earth that may pull him through. He told me his troubles, and this ought to be his salvation."

The powerful stimulants stirred a current of life in Saunders, and he heard and comprehended the tidings from "Shorty" Blake, and the heroic compromise of that distressed soul who had saved the home of his "pal," but could not let go his grip on the remainder of the windfall. The invalid gulped and there was almost the shadow of a grin in his stammering whisper:

"That b-b-blamed fool Shorty is a ——— angel, ain't he? I-I don't b-believe I'm d-dead yet. Say, can I go home if I'll get strong enough to stand the hike?"

This effort exhausted Saunders and he slept awhile. The surgeon was taking his pulse when he awoke, and the friendly nurse holding a cup of beef tea to his lips.

"You seem to have quit making an ass of yourself," said the surgeon; "and I've seen your company commander this afternoon. If you can work up enough strength to stand the trip to the coast, I'll see that your discharge papers are made out. You'll be no more good to the army."

The same inducement had previously failed to interest Saunders, but now he had determined to live, in the mighty inspiration of joy and hope renewed. He drank beef tea and begged for more, and when he flashed a feeble sputter of profanity because he was not allowed a bit of bacon, the ward became noisily cheerful. The captain of P Company was not a hard man, but he had suspected Saunders of malingering until the major-surgeon told him the private's hospital history, and how he had been saved from death by the miraculous intervention of the departed and flagrantly notorious "Shorty" Blake.

"Saunders isn't a bad soldier," said the captain, "but he's always been a bit too sentimental and broody. And if he's decided to save another funeral in the company, you'd better ship him home before he changes his mind. We can't feed him on another batch of such stimulating news if he slumps again. I'll look after his discharge papers, if you will certify him for disability."

It was three weeks later when Saunders, very thin and somewhat wobbly, waited in Nagasaki for the next transport homeward bound from Manila. He met a discharged corporal of Riley's Battery whom he had seen in hospital, and the gunner was eager to tell a highly colored tale whose peroration ran:

"And I was just in time to see the finish of 'Shorty' Blake's bombardment of Nagasaki, and it must have been a wonder all the way. They took him off to the transport in a sampan, with four little Jap policemen sittin' on his head and chest, and him kickin' holes in the cabin roof. The only night I was out with him he was playin' a game of turnin' rickshaws upside down, and sittin' on the axle, with the passenger yellin' murder underneath until Shorty got ready to move on. I asked him where he got all his money for rum and police court fines, and he was that twistified with booze, he says:

"'I ripped the mortgage off the old homestead like the hero in a play, and took my commissions like J. P. Morgan reorganizin' a railroad. If you don't believe it, ask the Jap whose name begins with a jade teapot.'"

# CAPTAIN ARENDT'S CHOICE

His wife half raised herself from the couch which had been her abiding place for more than twenty years. "My broken flower," the captain named her in his prayers at sea. The One to whom these petitions arose each night his liner throbbed along the Western Ocean track had granted that the heart and soul of the wife should wax in strength and sweetness while her body lay bound in chains of suffering. Because to-night there was worry in the tired, brave eyes which strove so well to mirror only gladness when the captain was at home, he was much disturbed, the more because he had made the cloud to come.

She looked, indeed, like a "broken flower" beside the towering strength of the captain, who growled through his flaming beard when he would speak most softly, who moved in a series of small earthquakes as he tried to pace with gentlest tread, while they thrashed out the momentous problem.

"To think of the new home is wonderful," she said in German, for this they talked when together. "Do the doctors truly believe I shall be stronger if we live at New York? Is there, indeed, hope of health again? Ah, but it is risking all we have saved in these twenty-five years, and——"

The captain no longer withheld his voice and it boomed through the little house with a hurricane note, though he meant it to be only reassuring:

"But the gain is wonderful. Such a home as I have found last voyage—in the country, in the hills, near New York. There is life in the air, and it will make you well every day. And better than that, what is everything to you and me, I shall be with you almost a whole week every voyage—almost a week in a month. Now, when I must sail from Liverpool, I am home here in Antwerp with you perhaps two days a month, perhaps not at all when storm and fog delay my ship, or when the passage is bad for the North Sea packet in winter.

"The doctors say you cannot live in wet, gloomy England, and here it is not much better. You will get well where we are going. We can be together as much as when I was chief officer in the old *Deepdale*, running out of Antwerp. The deeds of the home are ready to sign. I pay the ten thousand dollars when I come to New York this voyage. Then you come out the voyage after with me, for the company makes for us exception to the rule that a wife cannot sail on her husband's vessel."

She wistfully smiled as if led by a beautiful dream, thinking in her heart that to be sure of seeing her husband so often would be more than ever she dare hope for. Even beckoning health must yield first place to such a gift as this, but not yet satisfied she asked with tremulous insistence:

"But the bank will send the money over without risk, and it is all we have in the world, dear Max. Do you remember how the nest-egg was put away so long ago, when we hoped for children, and this was to be the beginning of their fortune? Why carry the money on your ship? Why take it with you?"

"*Mein Gott*, sweetheart mine, is not the old *Wasdale* safe as the dry land? Is not the old vessel safer than the banks, which, as they say in New York, bust higher as a kite every little while? Perhaps they give me a piece of paper worth ten thousand dollars in Antwerp. When I dock in New York, perhaps the bank has gebust while I am in mid-ocean, then my paper is worth nothing; the money is a total loss. In the *Wasdale*, in my room, in my safe, it is mine, and I have never lost a life, much less ten thousand good dollars. You do not worry when I go to sea. Am I not worth as much as our stocking full of gold? Answer me that, my Flora."

He did not know through how many nights, when she heard the winter gales from the North Sea cry over the roof, a quivering agony of fear had gripped her wide-eyed lest the *Wasdale* might have met disaster. But experience had taught the wife that no argument could prevail in which the safety and strength of the ship were questioned. Helpless to make reply, she accepted defeat, for the parting hour was far gone and the separation always taxed her fitful energy near to breaking.

Always as he raised her for the last kiss, and then halted reluctant in the doorway, he was to her as her bright youth had first seen him, a red viking, born to master steel and steam instead of the galleys of his forebears. This night he smote his chest resoundingly before he vanished into the hallway, and said in comforting farewell:

"It is here, in the old brown wallet, next my heart, where thou dwellest, my Flora. Our money is soon on the old *Wasdale*. God keep you!"

---

The biting wind of early March fairly whipped the captain up the side of the liner lying, with shortened cable, mid-stream in the Mersey. Clutching a stiff hat with one hand, baggy trousers fluttering, the tails of his frieze ulster tripping him, it was an odd and ungainly figure of a man that gained the deck and lumbered forward. A quartermaster near the gangway grinned when the pot-hat bounced from the bristling red head and carromed merrily off the deck-house, but a glance from the tail of Captain Arendt's eye froze the mahogany countenance of the offender into instant solemnity. It was a hint that the master of the ship was coming into his own. A few moments later he emerged from his quarters transformed. The smartly setting uniform of blue and the flat cap jammed down hard were so evidently what he belonged in, that the shore-going clothes had been like a clumsy disguise. A small boy flattened himself against the rail and saluted with immense dignity. The captain pinched him with a hairy paw and chuckled:

"Hello, Moses, or vas it Josephs I calls you last woyage? Holy Schmokes! If you keep my room no better dis woyage, I bites your head off close to your neck. You hear? Scoo-o-t."

"Moses-Josephs" fled, and Captain Arendt turned on his heel to go back to his room, remembering with a start that he had not placed the precious wallet in his safe, but had transferred it to his blouse. He clapped his hand to the breast pocket, hove an explosive sigh of relief when he found it there, and was instantly bent on banishing all chance of loss, when the chief engineer popped up from below and sought him out in breathless haste with these tidings:

"Sorry to trouble you, sir, but a drunken dock-rat of a Liverpool fireman refuses to go on watch, and he's reinforced the argument with a slice-bar, and laid out two of my oilers and a stoker, and I need more help to get him in irons. He's raising hell, and no mistake, sir."

The captain was halfway down the ladder before the chief had done speaking, and despite the bigness of him, made his way to the fire-room like a squirrel. The pallid, sodden mutineer, backed into a corner, was swinging the iron bar in empty circles, fighting the dancing shadows from an open furnace door, cursing and muttering. His bleary vision had no time to focus on the big man with the red face and snapping blue eye, who ducked under the weapon, smashed him in the face with one hand, squeezed his neck in the other, and flung him against a bunker door with such force that he lay as he fell, a dirty, huddled heap.

"Vash him off on deck, and put him in the hospital," said the captain. "He's a goot man ven sober. He vas vit me in anudder ship once. I knows him. Only his ribs is cracked, I t'ink."

When the five thousand ton *Wasdale* began to crawl down the Mersey, a hundred emigrants clustered along the after-rail, and shivered as they chattered. Two score cabin passengers walked the saloon deck amidships, and watched the great gray docks slip past. Twilight brooded over the Irish Sea and the filmy Welsh coast when dinner called them to make swift acquaintance, from which the ponderous good humor of the captain was missing. He dined alone in his room, and hastily, because he preferred to keep close to the bridge in these jostling waters. Yet the night had become almost windless, and so clear that the twin lanterns of the light-ship off

Carnarvon Bay gleamed like jewels on a canopy of black velvet. Captain Arendt leaned on the rail at the end of the bridge, and sniffed the sparkling air as the evening wore late.

"It looks goot," he muttered; "but I schmell fog. Yes, I schmell fog, and the rail is schticky, and the paint is schticky, and dere will be fog before morning."

He rubbed a massive shoulder and turned to the chief officer:

"And my rheumatism tells me dere vill be wet fog. I am coldt, and vill change my coat. I am also an old fool; but tell the engine-room to stand by for fog, not before morning, but before midnight, by Chiminy! I schmelled it strong dot time, and I never schmelled him wrong."

"Moses-Josephs" was caught in the act of brushing and laying away the captain's shore togs with absorbed attention to detail.

"Choke dot vistlin' noise off, and run avay," was the order that sent the boy scurrying toward the door. "Vait, I tells you," halted him as if he had fetched up against a wall. "How is your mudder, boy? She was pretty sick last voyage, you tells me. Better? Dot is fine. When we come again to Liverpool, if you are a goot boy, you can lay off one trip mit wages, and help her get well. Now scoo-o-t. I don't want you around. You is a tamned nuisance."

"Moses-Josephs" ducked in thanks, and the captain locked the door behind him, and sat at his desk with the "old brown wallet" before him. "I vill count him once," he confided to the barometer, "for fear he may have ewaporated while I forgot him."

His glance fell next on the picture of his wife, framed in silver against the wall. As he slowly counted the rustling notes, he talked aloud to her in German, as he had done many times in sheer loneliness and longing:

"Four hundred pounds—the first four hundred pounds came hard, my Flora, didn't it? Ten years we saved it while I was fourth and third officer in the company. One thousand pounds—we had a grand celebration when that was landed high and dry, eh? Fifteen hundred—it is a grand investment this. Two thousand pounds—it is a fine fortune, but we would be rich with nothing."

The square-hewn face softened and the flinty blue eye was misty as the captain bundled the notes into the wallet and stooped to open the little safe beneath the desk. The combination, always puzzling for him, was unusually tricky, and as he wrestled with it the speaking tube whistled near his ear.

"There's thick fog ahead, sir. We'll be into it before long," rumbled the voice of the chief officer from the bridge.

The captain hastily thrust the wallet into the top drawer of his desk, wriggled into a heavy reefer, and went on the bridge. A dense belt of darkness hung low ahead on the water and curtained the stars. Presently this barrier strangely streaking the clear sky was changed to dirty, gray clouds, then into blinking mist. Thus the fog shut down like wool.

The lamenting whistle of the *Wasdale* at once began to protest against this game of hide-and-seek. The bridge indicator signaled "half speed," and the vessel stole ahead as if in nervous dread, like a blind horse in a crowded thoroughfare.

Before long she began to feel her way with frequent pauses, while those on watch, from bridge to crow's nest, listened, listened. Their eyes were useless; their ears dreaded lest they hear too loud reply to the siren that shouted over and over again to this world of gray nothingness that the *Wasdale* was abroad. The ship crept ahead, slowed to listen, crept ahead again, but the responses to her outcries so soon became softened or silent that they held no menace.

The hour was near midnight. In their staterooms, the cabin passengers awoke to cast sleepy abuse at the fog-horn, and turn over again to slumber, warm and dry, believing themselves as secure as in their own homes. On the bridge an uncouth, dripping specter in oil-skins suddenly threw back his head and spun round to face the starboard quarter as if he had felt the sting of a bullet.

A moment's waiting, the fog-horn of the *Wasdale* moaned again, and from out in the baffling pallor came the ghost of a reply, nearer than when last heard, louder than when its previous warning had startled the captain.

The other steamer, groping to nose a clear path through the hazards of these waters, steadily became more clamorous.

The *Wasdale* called with loud, imploring blasts as if asking the stranger to speak more distinctly. The chief officer said as he glanced at the helm indicator:

"She's barely got steerage way now, sir."

"Let her go as she is for a liddle bit," replied the captain. "Dot feller is going up channel, I t'ink. But vat he do heading our way in such a devil of a hurry?" For a deadened hoot told that the unknown was drawing close aboard. The straining eyes on the *Wasdale's* bridge could see not more than two ship-lengths into the midnight fog.

"It is like dot game they play in the steerage," was the captain's whispered comment. "Two fellers is blindfold, and the udder sundowners make 'em chase one anudder round the deck."

The warnings from beyond had assumed definite direction, as if the stranger were guided by a fell instinct beyond the ken of her own officers. The *Wasdale's* siren ripped the night with quavering exhortation to hold hard and beware.

Suddenly the captain gripped the bridge rail and lifted himself on his toes with a smothered "Gott!" that was wrenched from the depths of his broad chest. Two lights blinked, red and green, almost abeam, and between them a towering mass dead black against the shrouding night, while amazed voices were heard screaming a flurry of orders from the fog, even before the roar of both whistles sounded a belated duet.

Captain Arendt was at his indicator with a leap and was like to pull the handle from its sockets as he signaled to reverse his engines, while his chief officer was shouting down the tube the same momentous summons. The third officer was softly treading a little jig-step, in a frenzy of impatience to have the thing done without more suspense. The *Wasdale* groaned and trembled to the furious reaction of her screw, lost headway, hung helpless, and showed a fair broadside to the assault of the other ship, which, wholly at fault, had begun to swing in fatal blundering, as if trying to pass under the *Wasdale's* stern.

The blow came, therefore, a little abaft the bridge. Succeeding a prodigious crash and rending of plates came a moment of impressive stillness, as the *Wasdale* tried to right herself from the shock, and then a foolish clatter of falling china and glass.

"He's waltzed clean through our pantry," said the third officer to himself.

Captain Arendt had only to rise from the planks where he had been flung, to command a bird's-eye view of the disaster. He looked down on the crumpled bows of the other ship, driven twenty feet into his own saloon-deck, and making a trumpet of his hands, shouted across to the other bridge, on which he could see figures moving like agitated black smudges:

"You is cut us half in two. Keep going ahead. Don't back out, vatever you do. Keep the hole plugged until I gets my peoples off."

The other ship seemed to hang as if wedged in the gap she had made, but before the officers of the *Wasdale* could reach the saloon deck the hideous, rending noise was renewed. The black bows of the stranger wrenched themselves loose, slid clear, and with a sobbing roar the sea rushed in as water falls over a dam. The withdrawn mass ground alongside, tearing woodwork into kindling, and then began to melt softly into the fog. Captain Arendt clambered back to his bridge, shouting as he ran:

"Ship ahoy, you! You have sunk us. Stand by to safe life. Get out mit your boats. Blow your vistle. You pig swine of a ———!"

Without reply the slayer faded like a phantom and was gone. From far down in the *Wasdale's* hold came a sound which made her captain thrill to feel that discipline had stood its first grim test. Collision doors in bulk-heads were grinding shut with the mutter of far-off thunder.

The electric lights on deck and in the saloons had been snuffed out. The ship was in darkness almost everywhere. From staterooms came screams of women and the wails of little children. The few stewards on watch were first to join the seamen on deck and those who had been flung from their bunks forward by the shock of collision. Into the ruck began to pour firemen and coal-passers from below, already flooded out of their compartments. It was perhaps three minutes before a welter of men began to flow in eddies toward the boats.

Meantime a wonderful thing was being done. The compelling personality of one man rose dominant as if he had been given the strength of ten. Panic was on tiptoe, ready to make an inferno of these decks, when it was routed because a hundred and forty men in the *Wasdale* had learned by the hard drill of experience that what this man said must be done on the instant. Captain Arendt called for light, and four sailors came running with the globe lamps snatched from the steerage and the wheelhouse. He swung one of these over the hole in the ship's side, and there was no need to wait for the reports of those sent below to make examination. Her bulk-heads could not save her, and she was settling fast.

"The old *Wasdale* vas not built for this," he said to the chief officer. "She will sink in one half hour—no longer. We must safe life. Get the men to their stations at the boats, joost like boat-drill we have every woyage. If they don't go, shoot 'em. But they vill go. I knows. Send an officer in charge of some goot men to handle the steerage."

The captain passed his own cabin door three times in the next handful of seconds. It was only a step, only an instant snatched from this priceless flight of time, to save the wallet in the top drawer of the desk. Each time he passed the door the desire to enter pulled him as if strong hands clutched his shoulders, but he went on.

Once he hesitated, and just then a grimy figure rushed past him headlong, and flung itself at the falls of the nearest boat, tearing at the canvas cover with teeth and nails, moaning as if hurt. At his heels came three others from below decks, knocking down all who blocked their escape. The captain tore their leader from the boat, and, like a red bear, seized him around the waist and tossed him overboard like a bundle of rags. Those near heard the choking yell of a drowning man.

The captain turned, and for the only time shouted at the top of his great voice:

"Men, the ship is in a sinking condition. The only coward on board vas gone. To your stations. We must all safe life."

A group of stokers huddled near the rail dropped the bundles of clothing they had brought on deck, and one of them, whose head was bound in rags, cried back:

"We're wid ye. You near kilt me to-day, you big Dutch —— ——, but by —— ——, you're a man. All right, sorr; we'll go after thim dummies in th' steerage."

It is consistent with few narratives of disaster at sea, but there was no more shouting among the crew of the *Wasdale*. They bent fiercely to their business, with whispers and muttered directions. It was not the nearness of death that stifled their outcries so much as the imminent neighborhood of a man with a stout heart and a cool head, who had hammered iron-fisted obedience into his crews through a stormy lifetime at sea.

The *Wasdale* had cleared with three hundred men, women, and children on board. There were boats to hold twice that number. It was only a question of time in which to stow these precious cargoes, a race with the sea which each moment sucked the *Wasdale* lower, as her decks sloped with a sickening list to starboard. A minute bungled meant many lives lost.

The captain seemed rather to drift than rush from one part of the decks to another. Going down the saloon stairway, he found a line of stewards passing passengers up as if they were so much baggage. The water was in the staterooms and washing along the alleys. Weeping women, clad only in their night-clothes, were shoved into cork jackets, bundled above, handed to the waiting seamen, and laid shivering in the boats without touching foot to deck. After ransacking the rooms to search out all the cabin people, the captain returned on deck to find confusion and some outcry where he had left an orderly flight to the boats. A white-faced passenger was on his knees, arms raised on high, his mouth contorted in trembling and husky appeal:

"We are doomed, and prayer alone can save. The ship is going down, the ship is going down, and we must be lost forever unless we gather in prayer. Come round me, and let us pray together. Oh, make a last appeal to your Maker to forgive us, before we go to meet Him with sin-stained souls. Man can do nothing, God can do all. Oh, save us, save our lives, we beseech Thee!"

A dozen half-naked passengers wavered, broke away from control, and fell around him, sobbing or trying to join in broken prayer. The voice of the suppliant rose to a shriek, and some of the crew balked, as if panic were stealing among them. Captain Arendt crashed through the pitiful circle and thundered:

"Choke dot idiot performance. Let the vimmen do the prayin'. Tumble into dot boat, you. You vill make the devil to pay here, I tells you. Be still!"

Fear had made the wretch deaf to reason. He subsided only to stagger to another corner of the deck, where his prayers again drew after him many who were convinced that death was inevitable.

"Jam him into the boat, and set on him," was the captain's order. "Break him in two pieces mit an oar if he makes one more yell."

Twenty minutes after the collision, the saloon deck of the *Wasdale* was only a few feet from the sea. The cheering creak of the falls as they ripped through the sheaves was sounding from one end of the deck to the other, as the boats descended while the captain counted them and held his breath, lest some unlooked-for lurch of the helpless ship should crush them against her sides like so many egg-shells. Were all hands out? He did not know, but it was time to leave. Some one jogged his elbow, and he turned to see little "Moses-Josephs," who said with trembling lip:

"I'm all ready to go when you are, sir. Anything more I can do? I took care of the stewardess and her cat, sir."

"Joost run to my room quick, and get the pocket-book in the top— No, stay here mit me. Yump into Number T'ree boat this minute, you liddle nuisance."

"I cannot let him go," groaned the captain, "and risk the child be drownded. Vat his sick mudder say to me if he don't come back?"

Surely there was time for the captain to rush up to his room, only half the length of the deck, and rescue the savings of his long life at sea. The wistful, troubled face of the wife as he had last seen her, the hope of home and health, fairly drove him to run forward with head down. He looked overside as he ran, and the gray sea was lipping so close that he could have touched it from the deck below. The planks under his feet rolled once with a weary, sluggish heave. He had once been in a sailing vessel which foundered in such a smooth sea as this, and he recalled that just before she plunged under there had been a series of these long labored rolls as if the ship were gasping for breath before the sea should wholly smother her.

He had almost gained the ladder to the bridge when he saw a moving blotch of white almost hidden behind the bow of a disabled boat. Swerving, he found a woman, a little girl, and a man, plainly their husband and father. The man was leaning over the rail, trying to call to the nearest boat, which was warily pushing away from the sinking ship. Spasms of fear so clutched his throat that his cries were only whispers, as one shrieks without voice amid nightmare perils. The woman clung to his coat, the little girl to her mother's garment. Evidently they had been overlooked because of the hiding place to which the man had blindly led them. As the captain reached the rail, the man tore himself loose from his wife and child with a great cry, and plunged headlong overside, not into the sea, but into the boat, which, at great risk, had been pulled close to save the group. With a crash, he smote the metal gunwale and fell inboard.

"Did you caught that dirty loafer?" shouted the captain.

The voice of the fourth officer in charge of the boat bellowed:

"Yes, sir; but I think he's dead as a mackerel. He landed square on his head; and one of the men who's picking him up says his neck is broken. Shall we stand by?"

"Holy Schmokes, yes. Sving that lantern so you can see to caught the voman first."

It was not an easy task. Another uneasy roll of the deck told him that the *Wasdale* was in the death throes. The water lapped through the scuppers as she lurched back and down to port. There were only a few steps to the bridge, the room, and the old brown wallet. He worked with furious haste. The mother had sunk to the deck, fainting and inert. She had seen her husband desert her on a sinking ship; she had heard of his death below. Her arms had locked around the waist of the child, hardly more than a baby, whose wisp of a night-dress was tattered about its neck. The captain tugged at the mother's hands to free the child, for he dare not toss them over thus embraced.

Each second imperiled the lives of the three, and also the fate of the ten thousand dollars that "was safer in the old *Wasdale* than in the bank ashore." At length the captain wrapped the child in his reefer, and tossed her into the waiting boat with a warning shout. The mother was a wrenching weight to swing clear, but when she had followed, a cheer from the boat told him that she had been safely caught.

He wiped the sweat and mist from his purpling face, and muttered:

"I must safe life; I must safe life, my Flora, as long as she floats."

The *Wasdale* still floated, as if the old ship were prolonging the struggle in order that the master who loved her might yet save the fortune that meant so much to him. He picked up a life-preserver thrown aside on deck, slipped into it, and looked around him, now desperately bent on reaching the bridge, even though the ship should sink beneath him. Surely none else than he was left on board.

A blob of light flickered far aft on deck—a globe lamp such as the sailors had been working with. He saw it, and caught hold of an awning stanchion to steady himself. It must be only a sailor dutifully standing by, before getting away in the last boat. Surely he could take care of himself. Was it not enough that he, the captain, should have done all that could be expected of mortal man, more than almost any other commander had ever done, to save his passengers and crew, hundreds of them, from a ship run down and sunk in half an hour? Was he not justified, in sight of God and man, in saving his fortune, not for himself, but for the helpless wife at home? It was all they had, on it was built all they hoped for. He swayed in his tracks, as the warring motives pulled him this way and that.

"Oh, my wife," he gasped. "I must be the last man to leave the ship, or I must go down mit her. I cannot, no, by Gott, I cannot go to my room."

He fled aft as if the devil had tried to snare his soul. The sea caught at his heels as he ran, even on deck. Aft of the steerage deck-house, the lamp he had glimpsed was dancing in crazy circles, where two firemen were struggling with a heap of Hungarian emigrants, who violently refused to help themselves. One of the would-be rescuers, whose head was bound in rags, spoke as the captain drew near:

"Don't hit me agin, sorr. Me ribs is stove in, an' I can't be handlin' these loony Dagoes in proper style. We had 'em all in the boat, sorr, but they swar-r-med back unbeknownst after their filthy bundles of duffle."

The emigrants were, indeed, difficult to pry loose from their huge packages of clothing, and as the disabled fireman was of little use in the pitched battle raging, his comrade was unable to wrest himself free of the frenzied men whom he was trying to save. The great strength and weight of the captain piled into the tangled mass like a battering ram, and one by one the reinforced firemen pitched the foreigners overboard to be fished out by the boat that lingered perilously under the counter.

"Yump yourselves!" yelled the captain; and as they dove, the stern of the *Wasdale* reared and seemed to be climbing skyward. Her commander cast one hungry glance toward the bridge, and saw her bows vanish in a smother of foam. As he jumped, he felt a shudder, as if every plate was drawing from its rivets. When his head rose on the crest of a roller, a boat-hook was twisted into his shirt, and he was yanked inboard by half a dozen hands, while the seamen bent to the sweeps for life or death as they strove to pull beyond reach of the coming suction.

The boat was not more than a hundred yards astern when the *Wasdale* pitched again, rolled once, and vanished with a thunderous farewell as her decks blew up in clouds of hissing steam.

As if the killing fog had waited for this sacrifice, it began to lift until the scattered lights in the eight boats began to flock together and the flotilla lay waiting for daybreak. The captain knew not whether any souls had been left on board, and miserably impatient he longed for light to count them.

"It is a bad night's vork," he said to the bos'n at the tiller. "I haf lost my ship, and I may never get anudder. I haf lost all my money, and I vill not get him again, for I am too old. But I hope I haf safed all my peoples, and if dot is so, I tank Gott."

Before day came their rockets were answered, and a big steamer loafed sluggishly toward the clustered life-boats. When she hove to, it was apparent that she had been in collision. Her bows were jumbled back to her fore bulkhead, and it seemed a miracle that she had been kept afloat.

"It is the svine vat runned into us," said the captain, "and den runned avay. I vish a few vords mit her skipper."

When the crew of the *Wasdale*, scrambling up the Jacob's ladders, had hoisted the bruised and benumbed passengers aboard, the crippled vessel limped on her course toward Liverpool. She was an Italian tramp, inbound from South American ports, and her captain had a taste of regions even more torrid when interviewed on his bridge by the late commander of the *Wasdale*, who returned aft to find his people vainly trying to find shelter from the cold.

"Why aren't dose poor miserable vimmen in the cabins?" he asked.

"The cabins are all locked, sir," replied one of the men, "and the Dago cook won't let us in the galley to get something to eat."

"Break open the cabin doors, and pitch the Eyetalian swab out on his dirty head, and cook whatefer you find in this show," was the order, and these things were done on the instant. Coffee and hash were made by the *Wasdale's* cooks, and passed by the *Wasdale's* stewards, and the invaded cabins ransacked for whatever blankets and clothing might serve to warm the pitiable castaways.

A little later the crew of the *Wasdale* was mustered for roll call. Each department rallied to its chief. As down the lines of shivering men the

"Here, sir," ran without a gap, the captain found himself choking back the tears, for at the same time the purser made tally of the cabin and steerage passengers, and found all present, even to the silent figure under a tarpaulin of the man who had slain himself.

The crew cheered, and the chief engineer stepped forward and began:

"Beg pardon, captain, but when we remember the *Elbe* and the *Bourgogne*, we have a right to think——"

The captain silenced him with a gesture and left them. Now, first he could think of his own crushing disaster, which, in his thoughts, eclipsed the great deliverance he had wrought by grace of his own courage and loyalty. He did not see that he had done anything to merit praise, rather was his plight almost worse than if he had gone down with the *Wasdale*. Brooding and unnerved, he did not rouse himself until the battered tramp was in the Mersey, and then he sent a tug ashore with tidings for his company, bidding them meet and succor his helpless people.

The melancholy procession had filed ashore before he gripped his resolution, and, coatless and ragged, sought his superintendent to make report of what had happened. This interview was brief, for the formal investigation must wait the captain's written word. The superintendent was also a man among men, and he was silent for a little time, looking at the bowed figure of the captain, who sat with his tousled red head in his hands, thinking now of the telegram he must send to Antwerp. A few broken words had told the superintendent of the wife and the old brown wallet.

Finally the captain wrote this message:

*I have lost my ship and all our money, but saved every soul on board.*

He handed this to the superintendent, whispered, "Please send it to her," and started to go out of the office, he scarcely knew whither. The superintendent halted him, grasping the bruised right hand that hung all nerveless.

"You have much to live for, Captain Arendt, and more to be proud of. Don't think for one moment that the company will forget a man who can do such a night's work as you have put to your credit. You take my unofficial word for it, this is a cloud with a silver lining."

Shortly before Captain Arendt was ready to take train that night for the Harwich boat to Antwerp, a telegram was handed him. He read it with a smile such as made his haggard face seem beautiful:

*What care I, if thou hast saved thine honor and thyself? Come to me.*

*Flora.*

# SURFMAN BRAINARD'S "DAY OFF"

Ashley Brainard left the life-saving station and lounged across the wide beach on which the cadenced breakers tumbled green and white. Beyond the gentle surf the Gulf Stream dyed the sleeping sea deep turquoise. The curving coast line wavered in the glare of sunlight fierce as midsummer, and the little landward breeze was warm and fragrant. Barefooted, clad in a sleeveless jersey and a frayed pair of white ducks, Brainard dug his toes in the wet sand and stood scowling at an automobile that moved swiftly up the beach. He seemed to resent its jarring intrusion upon the brooding peace of the tropical landscape as if a personal grudge were involved. In truth he was angry with himself that he could not smother the sudden discontent born of the sight of this drumming, flamboyant chariot which had swooped down from the big hotel five miles to the northward. When the car became a swerving speck and then vanished beyond a feathery clump of cabbage palms, the youth turned back to the station muttering:

"Now that Tarpon Inlet has closed up, I suppose we'll be pestered to death with these silly tourists. But, whew! it was like getting letters from home to see my kind of people again. I'd forgotten what they looked like."

The lusty surfman rubbed his tousled head as was his habit when restless or perplexed, and focused his irritation on the red-roofed cottage in which hitherto he had found contentment.

"This life-saving business in Florida is all tommy-rot. Here it is the middle of winter, no ice and sleet, no storms, nothing you ever read about to fit in with this game. I'm due to take a day off and get away from it."

He flung himself into the house, past the surf-boat that filled the lower floor, and climbed to the airy living-room above. Jim Conklin, mending a cast-net on the piazza, called cheerfully:

"You don't look happy, Boy. I thought you'd be glad to see some of your gilt-edged pals again. Did they try to borrow money from you, or did they make fun of your clothes?"

Brainard growled with an air of petulance absurdly boyish for the fine-conditioned bigness of him:

"I'm tired of shooting life-lines across a pole stuck in the sand and pulling my back-rivets loose in the boat after imaginary wrecks. It's mostly dress rehearsal in this shack. And we sit around and tell each other the same old hard-luck stories until I'm going daffy."

Conklin's weather-beaten face twitched and a little protesting gesture showed that he was hurt. Commander of a big passenger steamer at forty, he had piled her ashore in a fog three years before, and the iron law of his calling had thrown him "on the beach" without another chance. Offered a berth as watchman on the company's dock, he could not bring himself to this degradation even for bread and butter, and he had come to the surface again as one of the Tarpon Inlet crew.

Brainard saw his thoughtless blunder and quickly added:

"I didn't mean that, old man. You know how much I wish I could help you get on your feet again. Forgive me, won't you? I haven't any real troubles. Only a frost-bitten pineapple patch that was going to make my fortune. But it will be bearing again in two years, and then I'll be on velvet. Those gay visitors made me a bit restless, that's all, just as you walk the beach for hours after a Morgan liner passes close in shore."

Bearded Fritz Wagenhals, the station-keeper, broke in with a sardonic chuckle:

"It is the same way when we haf canned sausage for dinner. I think myself back in Heidelberg already, where I haf taken my university degree twenty years ago. What is the matter mit you, Boy? Was it the homesickness?"

"No-o, not exactly," confessed Brainard with a slightly embarrassed smile, "but I seem to be the only one of the three of us who can lift the curtain and get a peep at what he used to be. It's my day off, and with your permission, Skipper Wagenhals, I'm going to break my vows and trail up to the gorgeous Coquina Beach Hotel for dinner. It sounds rash, doesn't it? No sign of bad weather, is there?"

The Keeper replied with a shade of doubt:

"The barometer is not so conservative as I would like to see him, and we are very due to catch a norther already. But I don't think the weather will break before next day or to-morrow. You haf been a good boy, and you will haf your fling."

Brainard hauled a steamer-trunk from beneath his cot and began to toss out apparel which had been hidden therein for two long years. He held up a dinner coat and caressed it, rubbed a pair of patent-leather ties with a bunch of cotton waste, and made obeisance to a crackling shirt-bosom. Memories crowded back, and the smash of his high hopes of fortune was forgotten. Ashley Brainard was among his own again, a famous stroke of the 'varsity eight, counting a host of young men and maidens among his friends and admirers.

His mad impulse sent a flutter of excitement through the station. The surfmen crowded around and were eager to help their butterfly emerge from his cocoon. Fritz Wagenhals said, as he picked up the shirt with reverent care:

"It is a privilege if you allow me the buttons to put in. I once wore him every night. My Gott, that was so long ago! Also it is good manners here to eat mit your knife, but not so at the Coquina Beach Hotel."

The bustle aroused lanky Bill Stebbins, who was sleeping outside in the sand. He hurried in to offer aid and counsel:

"Dad burn it, I was onst sheriff o' Dade County, Brainard, an' I reckon I got a right smart pull yit. If you git pinched foh diso'derly conduct, raise a yell, an' I'll come a-runnin'."

When Brainard announced that he had no intention of dressing in the station the disappointment was so evident that he yielded to the clamor, and consented to array himself for what Fritz Wagenhals called "a little drill, to see if you are all-ship-shape-put together, mit your standin' riggin' taut."

These embarrassments delayed the departure until late in the afternoon.

In his one decent suit of blue serge, which had been lovingly pressed by the station cook, Brainard swung his luggage as if it were as light as his heart. He turned once to look at the red-roofed station nestling close to the sand-dunes, and for a moment felt as if he were playing the traitor to those loyal big-hearted comrades of his. Every one of them had fought with adverse fortune, and, beaten back, met the odds with smiling faces. He was the youngest of the crew and the pineapple plantation would yet release him from his chosen bondage. On this "day off" he ought to be back in the clearing by the lagoon, "bossing" his one laborer, but he looked ahead, and his young blood thrilled at the thought of glimpsing his own world again.

Northward from the station the coast swept seaward in a bold curve which ended in a low point over which the breakers played in spring-tides. Just beyond the Point, Brainard came to the Inlet and crossed, dry-shod, the passage between ocean and lagoon which had carried a ten-foot channel three months before. Now he could see, three miles to the northward, the long pier and the clustered roofs of the great hotel buildings. He had often come thus far on patrol, but had always gazed at the glittering resort as forbidden ground until he should regain his rightful place among these pleasure-seekers.

Soon he passed through a noble avenue arched with palms, and came to lawns that almost lipped the sea. After the smarting dazzle of sand and ocean, this lush, green vista was like cold water to a thirsty man. Parties of golfers were drifting across the background; white and fluffy gowns gleamed in the shrubbery. But when the wayfarer advanced to the long hotel piazza the smartly voluble groups of men and women made him unexpectedly timorous. Obtaining a room, he slipped through the crowded and colorful corridor to the nearest elevator, oblivious that more than one woman turned to look after the stalwart youth whose handsome face was so darkly burned and whose wholesome vigor was no veneer laid on after a wearing season in club-land.

Brainard felt more like himself when he was dressed and had tenderly absorbed the cocktail whose perfections had haunted his long walk. He swung into the dining-room as if he owned it, and chose a table facing the doors where he could view the grand entrance of the actors in this extravaganza. Three young women near him were chattering of spring flittings to Lenox and Westchester, and of summer pilgrimages to Newport and abroad. He heard familiar names of people he had once known. Soon a hand fell upon his shoulder and he looked up to see the chubby face of his classmate "Toodles" Brown, who fairly roared:

"By all the gods! It *is* Ashley Brainard. You dear old fool! Have you been dead or in jail or did you just float in with the tide? Of course I'll sit down. I haven't seen you since we sailed my schooner for the Atlantic Cup three summers ago. Explain yourself."

Brainard held the hand that had gripped his and gazed with speechless joy into the beaming features of "Toodles" Brown. Then the surfman grinned as he said:

"Good old Toodles! Why, I have a cottage just down the beach beyond the Point. I'm too darned exclusive to mix up with this herd of get-rich-quick millionaires and gilded loafers like your fat self."

"Living down the beach in a cottage," gasped Mr. Brown. "I've been here two seasons and I swear I know every cottager on the island. I think you're a blessed old liar. Tell me all about yourself, Ashley. You've given us all the cold shake, you know."

Brainard explained with a boyish laugh:

"Well, you know I was down here shooting through Christmas vacation of Senior year, and I got the pineapple bee in my bonnet. There were millions in it, on paper. But Dad wanted me to cuddle down at a desk in town. I stood it for a year and you remember how I cussed. Then I said, 'The glad free life under the palms for mine,'—bucked clean over the traces, and bolted. I was beginning to dream of counting my coin, when one night in January the thermometer slid three degrees too low, and, bang, what a difference in the morning! It was a case of pineapple frappé. I was almost broke, but I couldn't throw up the sponge, and last fall there was an opening at Uncle Sam's life-saving station for a strong lad used to fussing around the water. And there I am drawing my little old forty a month and proud of it, until my new crop comes in. But, oh, Toodles, I *am* glad to see you, and for Heaven's sake, tell me all the news about everybody! I never could write letters. And I'm a God-forsaken exile."

Chubby Mr. Brown was too agitated to think of gossip as he blurted:

"You're clean crazy, plumb dippy. Let me stake you till your ship comes in loaded with pineapples. Ash, come back with me. I'm planning a six months' cruise to the Mediterranean, and I've simply got to have you. It's sandy of you and all that, but it's silly pride to think you must bury yourself down here until you win out. Let the cunning little pineapple plants work for you while you come back where you belong. You a life-saver! It's absurd!"

"They are all better men than I in our crew," said Brainard slowly, "and it's a clean, simple, husky life, and I never was so fit. But—well, I wish I hadn't taken this day off. It hurts a little to mix up with this sort of thing. No, I can't borrow money, even from you. To-night I go back to my cot and corn-beef hash. But let's go it while the evening's young."

This suggestion made Mr. Brown brighten and take heart. After dinner they strolled on the quarter mile of piazza facing the moonlit sea, and the scent of tropical flowers hung heavy around them. "Toodles" Brown was anxious to have Brainard meet what he called "the youth and beauty of our set," but his chum asked him to walk first as far as the beach.

The pier was almost deserted, for the wind was rising and a fine spray filled the air with chilling dampness. Brainard looked at the sky with a surfman's interested scrutiny. The moon was dodging among fast-driving clouds and the surf was beginning to boom on the beach with a heavy, sullen note. He recalled the station-keeper's warning of a "norther," but dismissed it because the lonely red-roofed cottage seemed half a world away. Silent for a little while, when he spoke it was with odd and painful effort:

"Have you—have you heard anything of Marion Shaw? I—I m-mean Mrs. Westervelt? Is she well and—and happy?"

Brown chewed his cigar for a moment before he responded:

"That is just what I hoped you might want to talk about when we came out here by ourselves, Ashley. I didn't want to open the subject, you know. Yes, I saw her just before she sailed for Italy two months ago. She went alone, old man. Westervelt's a beast. I don't know what she went through with him, but they've made a clean break of it for good. She didn't confide in me to any extent. But we talked old times, and after a while, well, she asked me about you, and I had nothing to tell her. I didn't even know where you were. And—hem—she wasn't looking at me at all, and she wasn't even talking to me when she said as if she were thinking out loud:

"'I'm so lonely. Oh, if I could see him just once!'"

Brainard leaned over the railing and stared into the troubled sea as he almost whispered:

"Is she going to get a—get a———"

"Yes, after waiting two years. Then she'll be free to———"

"And you're going to the Mediterranean in the spring?" muttered Brainard. "God, if I could only see her! Two years, you say? If I could only see her!"

Brown laid an arm across his chum's big shoulder and said coaxingly:

"You don't want to meet any of these girls to-night, do you? We'll have a good old talk in my rooms later, and I'll have you booked for my cruise before we part company. There's a gilded temple of chance back here on the lagoon where the little ball rolls round and round, and I have a strong hunch that the luck is running to the black, and also dallying with my pet numbers, fourteen-seventeen-twenty down the middle row. Let's amble over and see what's doing in the roulette mart."

Brainard welcomed the diversion, for his thoughts were all upheaved. When they entered the "Casino," the busy green tables, the rattle of ivory chips, and the tingling excitement pervading the eager throng of men and women awoke in the exile a gambling passion that had long lain dormant. Without conscious act he found himself fingering his little roll of bills while he watched "Toodles" Brown buy a staggering pile of five-dollar chips. Fighting with his desire, Brainard idly chose numbers here and there, and trembled when he saw his empty choices winning time after time.

The whirr of the ball as it sped round the edge of its gleaming disk, lost headway, hesitated for a heart-breaking instant and fell into its destined compartment, was fascinating beyond words. Presently a florid dowager withdrew with a gesture of peevish disappointment, leaving vacant a seat near the middle of her table. "Toodles" Brown was profoundly absorbed in his own gloomy run of luck, and paid no heed to Brainard's modest investment of twenty-five counters worth a dollar each.

The life-saver had little expectation of winning. This was a distraction, an excitement, a part of his rare "day off," and he hung breathless on the surging uncertainty of every play. He noticed that "Toodles" Brown had forsaken his "pet numbers down the middle row," and with a reckless impulse he placed five dollars on each of the trio. The croupier gathered in the stake as callously as if a large part of a surfman's monthly wage had not been lost in this heady plunge.

"I think a zero is about due, and it stands for my prospects all right," thought Brainard as he slid five chips into the space around the "single 0."

The purring ball was uncommonly coy, and Brainard felt his heart thumping while it wavered undecided. When it nestled into its chosen nook, the croupier sung out:

"The single 0 has it."

He pushed a hundred and eighty dollars in chips toward Brainard. The young man flushed through his tan. A wild hope had flared in his heart. He resumed his play with tautened nerves and a softened light in his frank eyes. Belated luck must fall along the "middle row" he thought, and he covered Brown's "pet numbers" with chips, in the squares, on the dividing lines and in the corners. "Seventeen" won, and he gathered in his spoils without trying to count them. Then he threw his chips at random, on numbers and on colors, and the blind goddess was strangely kind almost with every turn of the wheel.

"Toodles" Brown ceased playing and looked at his chum wide-eyed. Brainard was exchanging some stacks of chips for bills, and others for chips of higher values, until he was staking the limit allowed on a number.

"For Heaven's sake call it off!" whispered Brown. "It can't last any longer. Pull out while you're ahead, and let me count it for you. You've nearly two thousand here."

Brainard brushed him aside and feverishly sputtered:

"Don't bother me. I'm playing for the biggest stake in the world. This is my day."

He snatched a fat roll of yellow-backed bills from Brown, and tossed it across the table to the splotch of red. Presently the croupier droned:

"Twenty-four wins, and the red."

The cashier counted Brainard's stake, piled up bills of equal value and shoved the bundle across the table. With tears in his voice Brown begged him to quit as Brainard made one more winning plunge and turned to his friend with a hoarse cry:

"I'm through. Damn it, come on! Let's count the plunder. I've won my freedom."

A few moments later Brainard divided somewhat more than five thousand dollars into two rolls and stuffed them into his trousers pockets. As the two young men passed out of doors, they were startled by the uproar of the wind. The palm crests were whipping to tatters with sibilant lament, and the air was filled with their flying fragments. From the beach came the great call of a raging surf and the sting of spray driven inland. Once, during his cyclonic hours in the "Casino," Brainard had heard the rising storm cry over the roof, but its summons had been unheeded. It had vaguely reminded him of duty, but even now he thought only of his lawless wealth as he strode toward the beach while "Toodles" Brown galloped clumsily in his wake.

When they passed beyond the sheltering lee of the last hotel building, the might of the "norther" buffeted them breathless. Brainard staggered out to the pier and clutched the nearest railing lest he be blown overboard. The rain of spray was drenching his evening clothes as Brown tugged at his coat and strove to pull him toward the hotel.

"Let me cool off," shouted Brainard above the tumult. "I'm going home with you, I tell you, Toodles. I'm going to the Mediterranean with you. I'm going to Italy with you, God bless her! I'm going back where I belong, and the pineapples can go to hell. There's five thousand in my clothes."

Brown thumped him on the back and roared:

"Of course you are, and you deserve your luck. But if you love me, come out of this. I'm a wet rag and you're worse."

For reply Brainard fought his way out along the railing of the pier, and gloried in the night. It matched his own mood. Like the sea, he had broken the bonds that for so long had held him tamed and stagnant. He was drunk with the wine of life, and the storm could not drag his whirling thoughts back to the red-roofed station beyond the Point.

Then the helpless Brown yelled in his ear:

"Turn around, Ash. Over here to the north'ard. Great Scott, what can we do?"

Brainard jumped to the note of alarm in the appeal. The moonlight still spattered across the white-fanged water. Driving along southward, close in shore, they saw a schooner, now a somber blotch, now outlined against the smother that flung itself at her. She seemed to be coming head on for the pier. The picture seared itself into Brainard's very soul. It hurled him back from his glad world regained to the station where he ought to be. But he waited to see if she could clear the pier. In an agony of impatience he crawled out where the sea was breaking clean over the structure, far beyond where Brown dared to follow.

He watched the doomed vessel wallow as she fled before the "norther," watched her lunge past the end of the pier, hardly more than a hundred yards away. By the rifting moonlight he could see that her decks were a tangle of wreckage, her headsails gone or flying in ribbons. She was pelting straight down the coast, helpless to claw off shore, helpless to heave to.

This was what Brainard realized as he groaned:

"She's heading straight for the Point, and she can't be handled to clear it. Or they may be hoping to fetch the Inlet and get inside, and they don't know it's choked up."

As he ran toward the beach, Brainard wondered how he could have forgotten. Why had not the first note of the storm called him home?

He waved a wild gesture of farewell to his friend, and tore down the boardwalk promenade, past the great hotel whose hundreds of windows were ablaze with light. Inside he glimpsed many dancers, and an eddying gust picked up the strains of the orchestra and brought faintly to him the taunting sweetness of a waltz song, "Love Comes Like a Summer Sigh."

It was Surfman Brainard of the Tarpon Inlet Station that plunged off the end of the walk into clogging sand, for the tide had covered all the beach, and he must toil up as far even as the gullied dunes. He kicked off his hampering patent-leather ties, threw his coat after them, and limped over driftwood and gnarled palmetto roots, falling, scrambling, swearing in a frenzy of eagerness to join his comrades. The sand whirled in blinding drifts, and he rubbed his eyes to look for the laboring schooner which vanished in a little while as if she were blotted out.

He remembered that somewhere a road led back into the tangled live-oak and palmetto hammock beyond the sand-hills. With a shout of joy he dove through a gash in the tufted hillocks, and his bare feet found a wagon track in firmer ground. Now the storm wailed overhead, but in darkness that was almost rayless it twisted limbs from the tortured trees and tossed them in Brainard's path; it flung the meshed creepers across his way to trip him headlong.

"She's bound to fetch up a long way this side the station," he grunted, "and the patrol may be at the other end of his beat. And those poor devils can't live long in the sea that's smashing over the Point."

Then he thanked God for the fitness of wind and limb which had come of long months of hardy drill and plain living, for the Inlet was just ahead as he came out on the roaring beach. He looked seaward for a rocket, and shoreward for a signal from the patrol. No light showed anywhere in the gray night.

He splashed across the tide-swept bar, and when the bones of an ancient wreck loomed close by, he knew he was within a mile of home. A dark smudge moved against the white sand-hills, and he fell into the arms of Jim Conklin on patrol.

"Schooner's coming ashore," gasped Brainard. "She passed the head pier, heading straight down and helpless. She was in distress for fair. If she hasn't come this far, she's piled up on the Point. I'll go to the station while you find her and signal us."

Conklin said not a word, but made a bull-like lunge against the storm. When Brainard had roused out the crew, Fritz Wagenhals shouted:

"Our boat is no good for us on the Point. Get out mit the gun."

Six men and the cook stormed up the beach with the life-gun and tackle, and as they toiled through the heavy sand in the teeth of the wind, Brainard was near collapse. But he rallied when they crept out toward the Point, and a red Coston light sputtered and flared ahead. Then Jim Conklin ran back to them waving his torch and crying:

"She's in the breakers on the weather side of the Point. The Boy guessed right. Breaking up fast, she is. Hustle up the gun."

When they sighted the stranded schooner even Brainard, who had foreseen her plight, was amazed at the quick fury of her destruction. The black lump of her hulk lay in a surf which broke sheer over it, and the stump of her mainmast rolled in appealing gestures to the sky. The first shot was fired dead against the wind, and the line fell short. A second and a third failed, and they did not even know whether life was aboard the wreck. At last a quartering shot sent the line across the schooner, and there came feeble twitches, electric pulsations that sent their message to the men ashore as if hands had been clasped across the boiling inferno of white water.

The wreck was breaking up fast. Her timbers strewed the beach, and drifted menacingly in the surf. But with slow, halting effort, the whip-line followed the slender cord of the projectile, and after that the heavy hawser trailed out into the night until the jerky signal came ashore that all was made fast. The surfmen tailed on and the breeches-buoy was dragged shoreward. At length a sodden shape, coughing and groaning, was pulled up on the sand by the men who rushed among the combers. Four more trips the breeches-buoy made, and three more sailors were fetched ashore alive. The last of these was asked how many were left aboard and he gasped:

"Nobody but the skipper, an' he's hangin' on by his toenails."

On shore they waited in vain for a signal, and none came. It was more ominous when the hawser slackened. It was read as a death-warrant when the hawser yielded to the tautening heave of the surfmen, yielded with sickening ease and came washing and writhing in to them, hand over hand, broken adrift from the wreck. The little group on the thundering beach stared across the ghastly water at the dissolving lump of the schooner, knowing by instinct that it would be foolishly futile to shoot another line seaward. They waited, and it was all that they could do.

To young Brainard this suspense was more killing than all the stress through which he had furiously toiled. No light, no sign of life, nothing to tell whether or not death had won in the home stretch!

A rescued seaman, battered and spent, cried out from where he lay on the sand:

"Matt Martin his name is. The *Lucy B.* was the vessel's. Coal to Havana. Mate washed overboard last night. He's a good skipper, is Martin; looks like that youngster in the white shirt there."

"We'll find him at high-water mark in a day or so," bellowed Fritz Wagenhals. "My Gott, I wish—no, the boat is no good here."

The young man shot his fist seaward.

"I'll try to swim out with a line if you'll let me."

"No, you don't, you tamn fool Boy!" the keeper shouted back.

Brainard doubled along the edge of the beach like a hound baffled by a lost trail. He was almost beside himself with bitter anger at the storm that it should have wrought this cruel climax. It had come as a tremendous revelation to him that he could help to win this great fight against wind and sea. His splendid strength had some place in the world of deeds after all. Fierce joy and thanksgiving had thrilled his every fiber that in this hour he was permitted to be one of the Tarpon Inlet crew. Now to be robbed of the life of the captain of the vessel, to stand like wooden men and let him die who had stayed by his ship for duty's sake—this was more than profoundly sad, it was maddening.

Blindly scouting a little way up the beach, Brainard glimpsed a bit of wreckage rearing shoreward, carried beyond the other watchers by some freak of the undertow. It looked like all the other sorry fragments of the schooner, but a second glance showed him a white patch gleaming against the black timber. It might be the tattered foam, but a wild hope halted him in his tracks, and he stood staring at the tumbling mass. The white patch did not vanish, it seemed to move as if writhing against its background, and now he was sure he saw it move. To wait an instant longer was to see the bit of wreckage pounded in the surf as by Titan sledge-hammers. He tore into the first line of foam, head down, arms extended. A few tripping strides, and a wall of water crashed down upon him, solid and resistless. Stunned as he was he dove by instinct, and caught breath beyond the breaker. The fragment of wreckage to which something was clinging rode a few yards beyond him. Again he was flung down and tossed shoreward, and again he dove with fast weakening effort, nor could he see that behind him the other surfmen were struggling to reach him in a hard-gripped human chain.

*As he rose the jagged timber was hurled straight at him.*

As he rose, the jagged timber was hurled straight at him like a projectile. He tried to dodge it, flinging out an arm to clutch at something white half wrapped round it. A broken nail or bolt caught his clothing, and dragged him headlong. While he threw his arms about the timber he felt the rags of his trousers tear loose, and he shook himself free of the deadly hold. He was no more than conscious that something stirred as if alive beneath his shifting grip. Presently the surfmen cheered as they hauled ashore the broken beam from which they had to pry loose two half-naked, water-logged, but living men.

Day was breaking when the crew of the schooner, a full muster roll, were helped into the station. The weary surfmen gave their bunks to the rescued, and the black cook made strong coffee and corned-beef hash with incredible speed. Brainard fell on the floor like a dead man. But he could not sleep, for the night had been too crowded with racking events. His hurts and exhaustion were forgotten as the evening at the Coquina Beach Hotel came back to him, dimly at first, then focusing more sharply, as if he were recalling things far distant in time and place.

Amid this welter of impressions loomed the fact that magically the means had been provided for him to go back to his own, and more than this, to see her whose message had come as from the dead awakened. As if in a dream, he fumbled for his trousers pockets. Then it came to him that he had been forced to put on Jim Conklin's oilskin breeches while that comrade was half dragging him home from the wreck. He dully wondered why, until beneath the oil-skins he found a waistband and a few sodden rags, all that was left of his evening clothes. Pockets were gone, and with them——

"Five thousand dollars," he muttered in dazed, stupid fashion.

Just then a babbling chatter broke from the nearest cot. Brainard raised his head and saw a young man, no older than himself, sitting up and feebly swaying, his wits awry for the moment because of what he had suffered. The captain of the lost schooner wrung his hands and cried, while the tears were on his bruised face:

"No, no, I tell you, the *Lucy B.* was not insured.... I named her after you and she was a lucky vessel.... Cut away the rags o' that forestays'l, and we'll bend on somethin' that 'll hold.... We've got to heave her to, I tell you.... Five thousand dollars clean gone, all I've got and.... If we can fetch Tarpon Inlet before we founder, we can get inside.... The *Lucy B.* gone to pieces.... You're a liar.... Why, I just bought out old man Holter's share last voyage.... Five thousand dollars, all in the *Lucy B.*.... All I've got and——"

Brainard was moved to pity, then amazement, that in this fashion he should be brought face to face with a tragedy so very like his own. But he glimpsed the fact, and was ashamed of it, that he would be stirred to deeper sympathy for the young skipper if there were no womanish wailing over his loss. And then, guilty and remorseful, Brainard realized that his own heart was full of sullen repining, bitter discontent with the fate that had robbed him of his treasure and his hopes, futile outcry against his forced return to the life of the station. He, then, was wholly lacking in that very fortitude which he wished to see displayed by this broken, fevered sailor in the cot, whose misfortune was, by far, the more crushing.

Brainard crawled stiffly outside to be alone. For some time he painfully overhauled his surging thoughts, and slowly there faded from his tired young face the clouding trouble that he had seen mirrored in the face of the boyish captain. Then he said aloud as if it were a verdict:

"A man who can't take his medicine is a pretty tough spectacle, isn't he? And it was all a dream, yes, all a dream—of money I didn't earn, and—and of a girl I can't marry."

He looked through the doorway, saw Jim Conklin slip over to the captain's cot and stroke the hot forehead, and heard him say:

"I know what it is, old man. I've been there myself."

The touch of Conklin's hand seemed to bring the skipper to himself. His slackened mouth closed with the snap of a steel trap, and into his face came the alert and aggressive look of an unbeaten man. He smiled up at Conklin and said weakly:

"I must have been a little upset in my top story. Was I talkin' foolishness? Thank God, we're still alive an' kickin' strong. I'm all right. How are my men? No use crying over spilt milk, is there, shipmate? How's the kid that yanked me ashore?"

Brainard went to his side, repeating as if he were thinking aloud:

"There's no use crying over spilt milk. I dreamed I lost five thousand dollars last night."

"Well, I'll be jiggered, so did I," cheerfully responded the skipper. "But it wasn't no dream for me. It won't make a bit of difference a hundred years from now, will it? Vessel a total loss, but I'm no total loss, not for a minute. You fished me out, and thanks for a neat job, for I'm pretty fond of just livin'."

Brainard gripped the outstretched hand, and the two young men smiled into each other's eyes. Ashley Brainard was glad that he had found a man, but gladder was he that he had found himself. For in that moment the life-saver routed all his regrets, as he turned to Jim Conklin, with vibrant earnestness and shining face:

"I'm mighty glad of the chance to stay here for a while among you men. For I'm pretty fond of just living, Jim, even if my dreams can't all come true."